3MEN

1 WOMAN

Jennifer R Scott

Jennifer R Scott

Three Men, One Woman

---

http://CARRIBEANFICTIONJS@GMAIL.COM

Facebook: Jennifer RM

Instagram: Jennifer.rm.33

Acknowledgment- to my friend Donna, Marie, my daughter Shantelle and my son Shamar thank you all for your encouragement. All friends and relatives' names not mentioned, thank you all for your support.

Love is sweet, love is bitter
and love can also be deadly.

Who has the right to tell us
whom we can love?

Love does not see color.

Love is love.

This book is sweet, lovely,
inspiring, and surprising

PROLOGUE

D esaray!" John hollered in a desperate voice, "Please listen to me; go back to your mother's house. I do not trust this guy," John said.

"But the cleaning lady—"

John cut me off. "Desaray, just go," he pleaded.

"Okay," I answered. "I love you, baby."

"I love you too, honey," John responded.

WHAP!

I was stunned. "Oh my God! John, this guy just hit me!" I cried out.

"Desaray, get the hell out of there!"

WHAP!

I stumbled against the kitchen cabinet and fell to my knees, blood spilling from my nose. I yelled out, "John! Help me! He's going to kill me!" I started begging for my life.

"Desaray!" I could hear John yelling my name as I tried crawling toward the cell phone which had fallen out of my hand. Blood and mucus drained onto my white pants.

"Zander, please don't kill me; I am begging you," I pleaded with him.

I could still hear John screaming out my name as the phone was still on speaker. I curled up close to the refrigerator, trying to protect myself from the kicks Zander was raining down on me as my life started to fade.

"Zander, please don't kill me," I begged with every bit of strength I could muster. "I am sorry."

STOMP. STOMP.

"God, please… God, please don't let him kill me!" I cried out. *STOMP.*

"Please… Zander, please, do not kill me! I am begging you."

"You are begging me now?" Zander said with a sardonic laugh. "You think you are too good for me," he said in broken English. "I took care of this property and protected it, and now you think I am not good enough to stay here? Bitch. You think because you married a white man that you are better than me?"

STOMP. STOMP. STOMP.

Let us go back to the beginning…

CHAPTER 1

DESARAY

I was working at the Regal Hotel in Montego Bay. It was a magnificent European-style building overlooking the deep blue Caribbean Sea. The soft breeze that fluttered across the ocean swayed the pine trees back and forth. The smell of pines and jasmine lingered in the air. I inhaled the beautiful scent as I looked around at the beauty of the island, Jamaica.

I hurried to the maid's closet, gathered my cleaning cart, and changed into my uniform. My duties were to clean all the rooms on the ninth floor within my eight-hour shift.

I knocked on each door before entering. I made the beds, cleaned the bathrooms, dusted the furniture, and then quickly vacuumed before I moved on to the next room...

I knocked on the door, but no one answered. So, I walked in. I was not expecting to see anyone there. According to my work order, the room should have been unoccupied.

I was shocked when I bumped into a white man sprawled naked on the floor, showing no sign of life. He was of medium built with jet black curly hair. He looked like he belonged to one of those Italian mafia families I saw in the movies.

I rushed over and knelt beside him. "Are you ok?" I asked, shaking him.

After a few moments, he woke up and looked at me with dazed smoky grey eyes.

"Are you ok?" I asked again.

"I'm good," he responded. "I fell asleep on the carpet and didn't hear you knocking."

I helped him to his feet and slowly sat him in a chair nearby. "Do you need some water?"

"Yes, that would be nice," he responded.

I handed him a glass of water and asked if he needed me to get him something else.

"No, thank you, you have been exceedingly kind. And thanks for the water," he said.

"I am here to clean your room. Do you mind if I go ahead and do it now while you step out of the room?"

"No! Do not bother. Tomorrow you can come back and clean it. I will be out of here before you come around again anyhow," he said.

I noticed the sadness in his eyes. I still had fifteen minutes left, so I started a conversation with him, wanting to know why he was so sad. "Where are you from?" I asked.

"I'm from the UK," he answered.

"Where exactly in the UK do you reside?" I questioned some more.

"In Brixton, England," he told me.

"Can I ask you a personal question?

He looked curiously at me, and I hesitated, hoping he would not think I was too forward. I decided to ask him anyway, "Why are you here by yourself? Don't you have a family? A wife? Maybe some kids?" I reeled off all the questions in one breath, hoping to encourage him to discuss his troubles with me.

"I do not have any children, but I had a fiancé, and she dumped me for my best friend."

I was even more intrigued as to why his fiancé would dump such a handsome man. I know I would not. I smiled internally. "Do you wish to share what led her to be with your best friend?" I wanted to hear more.

"I am a Wall Street investor, and I spend a lot of my time trading on the stock market. My passion was making, money, and at times, I neglected to give her the attention and love she needed. She started hanging out with my best friend, and before I knew it, they started sleeping together. I could not put my finger on it, but she had started acting shady, especially when my friend Gerald came around.

"One evening, I decided to surprise her at work. I wanted to take her out to a nice candlelit dinner. I had booked a reservation at the Tapas Room, Brixton, one of the finest restaurants in London.

"I saw her walking out of the building and I was about to exit my car but never got the chance to do so. She ran right into the arms of a man who was waiting just outside the building, and they kissed passionately. He handed her the roses he was holding. Then they held hands and happened to turn toward my car. That was when I recognized that the man was my best friend.

"I was furious; I jumped out of my car, punched him in the face, and cursed him out. To my amazement, my fiancé ran to his rescue and told me off. She told me our relationship was over. I could not believe that she had run over to help my best friend and had the nerve to break it off with me just like that, with no explanation. I felt so hurt, even betrayed. The woman that I should have spent the rest of my life with had dumped me.

"I had previously booked a short getaway for both of us in Jamaica. After she broke up with me, I decided to come down by myself and have an enjoyable time. But as you can see, it has not gone to plan. I feel so lost and lonely without her. I am still reeling from the shock of her betrayal. I am hurting and I just needed to numb my pain and let it go away. This bottle of Jack Daniels was my only outlet," he gestured towards the half-empty bottle on the nightstand.

The conversation was going well, and I was so fascinated by his story that I almost lost track of time.

"I am sorry, Mr. Lawrence, but I need to clock out; my shift has ended."

"What's your name?" he asked me.

"Desaray," I said.

"It was nice of you to stay here and talk with me. If it is ok with you, can we exchange numbers, and maybe we could chat some more?" he asked.

I hesitated because I did not own a phone. I could not afford one because most of my earnings went towards helping my mother with her bills. A cell phone would have been too costly for me to maintain on my small salary.

"Why don't you give me yours?" I suggested. He gave me his number and his address in the UK. "If I am not able to call you, can we write to each other as pen pals?" I asked.

"That sounds like a plan," he responded. We said our goodbyes, and I went back to the linen closet. I put my cart away and clocked out.

The next morning when I got to work, I started my usual routine. I went to the laundry room, picked up my cleaning cart, and then went from room to room, making beds, cleaning, and dusting.

I knocked on the door to Mr. Lawrence's room, and again I got no answer. I entered, walked over to the bed, and started pulling sheets from the bed. I walked around to the other side of the bed and noticed an envelope lying on the floor.

I picked it up, and to my surprise, it had my name written on the front. My heart was beating a bit faster than usual. I was very curious and excited to see what was inside. I tore the letter open and pulled out the folded sheet of paper. Wrapped inside the folded sheet were fifty pounds in notes and a letter. I unfolded the letter and started reading it.

My dearest Desaray,

I am hoping you are the recipient of this letter. I took a chance and left it on the bed, with the hope of you finding it. I just wanted to thank you for your kind gesture.

I was so depressed last night. I took a couple of sleeping pills and I guess the combination of pills and alcohol; threw me for a loop and knocked me out cold. I am not a drinker just in case you are wondering.

I appreciate you taking time from your busy schedule to offer me a glass of water and to talk to me. You made me realize that there are still caring and kind people in this world. You have opened my eyes and I now have a new perspective on my life. For that, I am grateful to you.

I am glad that you and I met each other, even though it was under unpleasant circumstances. Ha, ha. But sometimes life throws us a curveball.

I hope that you and I can remain friends and stay connected. I am sorry that I was not able to get a phone number from you, but you do have my address.

Looking forward to hearing from you soon.

Sincerely,

John Lawrence

P.S. I left you a little token to say thanks for being there when I needed a friend

I felt so emotional after reading the letter that tears welled up in my eyes. It was truly touching. I was glad that John had enjoyed our conversation. I counted the money again, realizing that it was more than my weekly paycheck. More than enough money for me to buy myself a phone and a calling card. I also wanted to say thanks to John for his kind gesture.

It was the end of the week, and I was looking forward to enjoying my two days off.

The next morning, I got up early. I was excited about calling John. I knew he would be astounded, hearing from me so quickly. I went to the hair salon and got my hair done. Then I went next door to the cell phone store and bought myself a phone.

I took my new phone out of the box. This was my first cell phone, thanks to John's generosity. They have a saying in Jamaica that *sometimes small favors bring big rewards.* This was my reward.

"Thank you, God," I whispered.

I inserted the phone card in the phone and turned it on. It suddenly lit up. I immediately punched in John's phone number and waited nervously as the phone connected and started ringing.

"Hello," he answered softly.

"Hello," I responded.

"Who is this?"

"John, it's Desaray," I responded.

"Desaray," he repeated my name. I could hear the laughter in his voice. "You may not believe me, but I have been thinking about you," he said.

I laughed. "Really?"

"Yes, I do not know what it is, but there is something special about you. I can't stop thinking about you," he said.

"I have been thinking about you too," I said to him.

"John, I have to hang up; I don't have much credit," I said, trying to save some of my credit for the next day.

"Hold on a second, honey," he said to me.

I started blushing. I had a wide smile on my face and was glad that he was not able to see my expression.

We continued talking for another ten minutes about the things we enjoyed, such as eating out, watching a good action movie, and traveling. The conversation was going so well that I lost track. The call ended as my phone credit was finished.

The next day I bought another phone card. I just wanted to hear John's voice. I had butterflies in the pit of my stomach as the phone started ringing.

"Hello, Desaray," John's voice boomed through the phone. I could hear the excitement in his voice and hoped that he could hear mine also. "Desaray, it's so nice to hear from you again. I was going to call you, but you beat me to the punch. How was your day at work?" he asked.

"The usual," I replied. I wanted to tell him that I missed him, but I worried that he would think I was a desperate woman, missing someone I had known for only a week. So, I kept my thoughts to myself.

I was thirty years of age and John was forty-five, so he was fifteen years older than me, but I did not care about his age. I liked him.

"Desaray," John said in his sexy English accent, "I know it is costly to buy phone cards on the island, so I will call you. Don't spend your money on phone cards; let me take care of that," he said.

I was glad that he would do that for me because I had no more money to buy another phone card until I got my next paycheck. We spoke for a while longer and by the time we ended our call, my head was in the clouds.

I was beginning to feel something for John, and I was hoping that he felt the same way about me.

I dreamed of leaving Jamaica to make a better life for myself and provide for my mother and my brother, Steve. I loved them with all my heart.

We did not have a lot of money, and I was the breadwinner for my family. Steve did not have a consistent job and, my mother did not work. To make extra income, I braided hair during my free time. Which helped to cover my mother's bills.

"One day, better must come." I continued to speak this motto, hoping that God would answer my prayer one day soon.

I did not tell John that I was involved with someone else. I did not want to complicate things between him and me. I knew it was over between me and my boyfriend, Freddie, and had known that since I had first met John. I was fed up with the way he treated me. How could I call someone my man when I hardly saw him?

He visited when he wanted to have sex and behaved as if he was doing me a favor because he was helping to pay my rent. Everything had to be on his terms. He did not care about me or how I felt. Always showing up unannounced as if he were surprising me when really, he just never wanted to make any solid plans. What a joke our "relationship" was.

I had been a fool, subjecting myself to his abusive behavior. I knew I had to find a good reason to end our relationship. I was not sure how he would react to the news, but I was done.

That night, I decided to do a little investigation and found out through a mutual friend that my boyfriend had two children with another woman. With whom he was still in a relationship with.

Finding that kind of info out?! Ouch! That hurts! I was shocked and devastated that all this time he had been lying to me. Never once had he admitted that he had a family, even when I had asked him on several occasions.

This was the last straw. I was done. I was hurt, knowing that all this time, I had been holding onto a relationship filled with lies. This man pretended like his disappearances were work-related when the facts were, he was in a committed relationship with someone else.

I blamed myself because I had put up with it. If John had not come into my life, I would have kept up the pretense that nothing was wrong.

It was Friday Evening, and I had just gotten off the phone with John when Freddie showed up again, unannounced. I asked him if he was seeing another woman. Again, he denied it.

"What's with all these questions?" he asked, sounding annoyed.

"I am done with this relationship," I said.

"Desaray, what is this? Are you breaking up with me?"

"Yes, Freddie, all this time you have been two-timing me, knowing that you are in a committed relationship."

"Desaray, I have no idea what you are talking about!" he continued lying.

I pulled out the picture my friend had taken of them having dinner at a local restaurant and showed it to him. He laughed, saying that it was his sister.

"Freddie, I am done. You can keep your lies to yourself. I am through being with you. Just go ahead and be with your family," I cursed at him.

"So that is it, Desaray?" he said angrily.

"Yes, this is it." I snapped.

Freddie pushed me out of his way so hard that I fell right on my backside. He started to verbally abuse me in the worst way you can imagine. When he finally left, I broke down crying.

I looked at myself in the mirror as the tears trickled down my cheeks, trying to see if there was something wrong with the way I looked.

Why couldn't I find a nice man who would treat me with respect?

Men told me I was stunning, standing at 5'7 with brown cocoa skin and nice curves. My eyes, which I thought were my best feature, were slanted, with light brown pupils. I had a pretty face with high cheekbones, and yet I was still not worthy.

I continued talking to myself, trying my best to build up my self-confidence. After I finished crying, it felt like a load had been lifted off me. I was now ready to give John all my attention.

CHAPTER 2

John and I constantly remained in touch. I had learned so much about him and his past. I told him things about me also, but some I could not speak about. It may sound strange, but I considered myself as being in a long-distance relationship with John. We spent so much time talking to each other it felt like we were living in the same space.

Both of us talked about our aspirations; marriage and having children were most important to us. Even though these were just conversations, I was hoping that John would be the man for me. He was a very generous person and took care of me financially, even though he was living abroad. I was profoundly grateful for everything he had done for me.

A year passed since the day I met John, and we had been corresponding long-distances every day. John had asked that I visit him in the UK. He sent me an invitation letter and an airline ticket.

I was excited about leaving Jamaica, even though I was going to miss my brother and mother. This was going to be my first time visiting a foreign country and being away from them.

My mother said she was going to miss me, but she understood my reasons for wanting to leave. This was an opportunity for me to make a better life for myself. I had been dreaming of this day for an exceptionally long time, and I imagined all the things I would do when I got there.

It was 8:00 p.m. on Friday, December 18th, 2001, when I walked into the pickup area inside London Heathrow Airport.

My heart was pounding, anticipating John's reaction when we saw each other again after so long. I was hoping that the chemistry we had had over the phone would be even better in person. I was also hoping that he would still feel the same way about me.

I saw him before he noticed me. He was so handsome, and I admired him from afar. John told me he was five feet eleven inches tall, but he seemed taller to me; he had a nice physique.

As he walked briskly towards me, my heart pounded. He looked rested, unlike that time when I had found him passed out in the hotel room. Then, his appearance had been ragged. He was looking so much better now.

My excitement was so obvious as I hastened my steps to get to him faster. Suddenly, he noticed me, and with outstretched arms, John pulled me into an embrace and squeezed me tightly, planting kisses on my face.

I was nervous but also excited. He held my hand in his as we walked through the airport. I felt protected, and all my nervousness was gone.

Everything looked so different and strange; it was nothing like the airport in Jamaica. This airport was huge, crowded, and bustling with people hurrying in every direction.

We stepped out of the airport and into the night air. I was captivated by all the bright lights. I was freezing my butt off as the freezing wind whipped through my thin coat. I was amazed by the snowflakes falling from the sky. All the trees and houses were beautifully decorated with this white, dusty powder that fell out of the sky.

We pulled up to this nice cottage on the outskirts of town. John took my bags from the car and opened the door to his cozy place John's house was sparsely furnished; I could tell it could do with some feminine touches, and I was hoping that I could do that during the time that I would be spending there.

John showed me around and then asked if I was hungry. I told him that I was starving and in no time, John prepared us tea and sandwiches.

We sat at the kitchen table, sipping our tea, and eating our sandwiches. We must have talked for over an hour about my trip, my mother, and my brother. John mentioned that I never spoke about my father, and he was curious to hear about him. I explained to him that my father had left my mother when I was six years old, and my brother was only three years of age. We had never seen him since.

I expressed to John that I would love to one day be able to give my mother and brother a better life. He said if we worked hard together as a couple, we could make it happen.

Those words meant a lot to me because it told me that John was considering the possibility that we would be together eventually. I felt the same way too and hearing him say that put me at ease. It showed me that John was thinking about my concerns. At that moment I knew that he was the one for me.

I was beginning to feel drowsy after a day of traveling, and I could not keep my eyes open any longer. I told John I was ready to retire to my bed. John picked up my luggage, which was in the kitchen, and led me to the guest bedroom.

He showed me around and then kissed me good night and proceeded to his bedroom. I was glad that John was a true gentleman and allowed me to make my decision on whether I wanted to share a bed with him on my first night there.

The next few days were like a blur, and conversation between us was easy. During a week of us spending time together, I learned a lot about John's habits, and he did the same about mine.

On Saturday, John took me shopping for winter clothing. This was going to be my first Christmas in England, and I was thrilled.

John also gave me the honor in choosing a Christmas tree to my liking and all the decorations I wanted to go with it. I had such an amazing time, running through the store and picking out John's Christmas gifts, even though they were bought with his money. It felt nostalgic.

This Christmas would be an incredibly special one for me, especially because John and I would be spending it together.

I admired the beautifully decorated storefronts along Brixton Village Market, lit with string lights and Christmas decorations. I felt like a kid, being able to experience this moment with John.

After we finished our shopping, we stopped at Charley's Pub for a quick bite. We ordered fish and chips and two glasses of draft beer. The meal was delicious. I was developing stronger feelings for John but was shy about sharing them with him. I was hoping that he felt the same way about me.

Later that night, we sat by the fireplace and sipped warm Irish brandy from our mugs while cozying up to each other, enjoying the ambiance of the fireplace.

John ran his fingers along my face, looked deeply into my eyes, and asked what I thought about him, considering that we had been sharing a space for over a week. I told him; I was extremely comfortable being here with him.

"What do you think about me?" I asked John, hoping to judge his reaction. My eyes fixated on his nice lips.

"I love you, Desaray," he said in a sensual voice.

My heart melted! I had never had a man tell me that he loved me. However, I did not want to say the *love* word yet because I was scared. So, I just gave him a wide smile instead.

I was beginning to feel sleepy; the brandy was affecting me. Something else was happening to me also. I had this yearning deep in my love nest.

"Baby let's call it a night," I said to him. I did not want to sleep by myself, so I asked John if I could sleep in his bed.

John pulled me closer to him during the night, slowly caressing my back and kissing me fervently. It felt good. John's caresses were also stirring up all kinds of strange feelings deep within me, feelings I had locked away for over a year.

"Hmm," I moaned, enjoying the sensation and the feelings that were consuming me.

I kissed him deeply, enjoying the feeling as our tongues danced together. I ran my hands against his firm chest and continued exploring the rest of his body, curious to see what he was working with. This moment was intimate for us. There was no rush; we had all the time.

I found myself comparing John to my ex. Who constantly complained whenever we got together; He was always rushing and found excuses why he could not spend more time with me? I was never his priority. He would disappear for days, and when he showed up, it was the same bullshit. Slam, bam, and goodbye. He did not care about my needs, only his.

Being with John was refreshing. I was able to relax and enjoy the moment. John was different he treated me with respect, and he was not forceful—it was all on my terms.

"Make love to me, baby," I whispered.

John did exactly as I asked. He made enthusiastic love to me, awakening the feeling that I had never known existed within me. I had never felt such love and passion. I had never experienced such tenderness and kindness. But this man, John, showed me that it existed.

CHAPTER 3

Five months later, my life could not have been better. John showed me, love. He showed me how a man was supposed to treat a woman. I also taught John how to separate his work from his home life. We spent a lot of quality time together, and we would go on small trips in and around London. One of my most memorable was visiting Buckingham Palace.

As time went by, I fell deeper and deeper in love with John. I was finally able to meet his father and sister, who lived in Cambridge. John's mother had passed away about two years before we met.

I liked his family, and I saw another side of John in his interactions with his dad. They laughed and talked about football as if they were two best friends who supported two opposing teams. His sister told me not to worry about them; She said they always argued like that when it came to football.

My mother and I communicated regularly, and John spoke to her during some of our phone conversations. He had made quite an impression on her with his English accent. She told me she loved his accent and hoped that he and I would get married. That was my mother's biggest wish for me. She had never been married, and she wished for me to experience the things she could never afford.

I rolled over onto John's side of the bed, and he kissed me deeply. "Can I tell you something, Desaray?" He smiled widely as he stared into my eyes. "I am so happy, and I feel loved whenever I'm with you."

"I'm glad that I can revoke such feelings within you. You have also made me a happy woman, and I have no complaints."

"Desaray, I haven't been to church in a while. Why don't we visit today?" John said.

"I would love to, I expressed. John and I dressed in our nice attire for church. We wore color-coordinated outfits, his navy-blue suits matching mine. We drove in the parking lot of this huge church called Brixton Baptist Church. As we entered the church, I was in awe. It was the biggest church I had ever visited. A feeling of reverence immediately overcame me as I looked up at the huge stained-glass windows and the detailed architectural ceiling.

The pastor welcomed everyone who was in attendance and delivered his sermon about giving from the heart. His words earnestly touched me as I thought about my mother and my brother Steve. I knew that everything I did for them was always from my heart. And I knew that John did the same for me because he was always so generous to me. Although I was not able to give John financial gifts, whatever I did for John, was always from my heart.

After church ended, John introduced me to Pastor Brown. He was so down-to-earth and funny, especially when he asked John if I was "the one" and John started blushing.

"You don't have to give me an answer now, he said. But hopefully, the next time I see you in church, I will get an answer."

A few days later, I was sitting in the kitchen enjoying a cup of coffee and thinking deeply about my time in the UK, which was ending in a couple of weeks, as I had originally only planned to be there for six months.

I loved being here with John and could not imagine going back to Jamaica after living in the UK for over five months. I had so many mixed emotions. I did not want to go back to Jamaica. I was fearful in telling John that I wanted to stay and was even more scared of being disappointed if he decided he did not want me to stay here with him.

"What's wrong, honey?" John asked me. "You seem a bit distracted."

"I was just thinking that in a couple of weeks, I will be heading back to Jamaica," I said.

John took me by my hand and led me to the sofa, and sat down, still holding my hands in his.

"Desaray, let's talk."

I was not sure what he wanted to say to me, but I put on my poker face.

"Desaray," he started out saying, you and I corresponded for over a year. We have been living together for over five months. I have enjoyed your stay here with me. I have not felt so happy in years. Desaray, do you wish to remain here in the UK with me?" he asked.

I was not sure that I had heard him correctly, so I asked, "What did you say, John?"

He repeated what I thought I had heard a minute earlier.

I was overjoyed. I never imagined that this conversation would have ended so well. "I would love to stay here with you, John!" I blurted out, feeling relieved.

A week later, we went down to the local registry office and got married. This would allow me to live legally in the UK, and not be fearful of being picked up by Immigration Enforcement (IE) and deported back to Jamaica.

John promised that eventually, he would give me a nice intimate wedding and a diamond ring. He explained to me that he wanted to do it the right way, but because of my situation, we had to get married immediately.

I understood what he meant, and I told him I was okay with the zirconia ring he had given to me and reassured him that our love was worth much more than a ring.

CHAPTER 4

Two years had passed since I started living in the UK with John. Our relationship was going great. We were falling in love increasingly each day. We were like love birds; we could not keep our hands off each other.

I started thinking that it was time John and I sat down and discussed my future—finding a job and going back to school. As John's wife, I wanted to contribute towards our household expenses and take some of the financial strain from him.

"John!"

"Yes, honey?" he answered.

"You and I need to talk about our future. I have been here for over two years now, and I need to do something with my life," I said.

"What do you have in mind?" he asked.

"I want a career. I want to go back to school and educate myself. I want to be able to work and contribute toward our bills," I explained.

"Desaray, everything is going great with us, and I am quite capable of taking care of you and all our bills," he said.

"I know, baby, but I want to work and feel like I am a part of something, not just be a kept wife."

"Desaray, did you forget what I do for a living? I am an investment banker, and I am capable of taking care of us."

I was not letting up on this conversation; I wanted a career, and John needed to let me make that decision.

John realized that he was not going to win this fight, so he eventually asked if there was a particular profession, I would be interested in.

"I want to be a hairdresser," I said. Women love their hair; it is their beauty. There will always be a demand for hairdressers," I explained.

"Ok, let me think about it and get back to you," John responded.

Another month passed, and John and I did not speak again about me going back to school or working, and I just left it at that. John gets so involved with his work and tends to forget about things we discussed and things that were important to me. I reminded John that these were the trivial things—like lack of communication—that broke up relationships. I did not want us to end up there.

My birthday was on August 24th, and I was trying to plan how I wanted to celebrate my big day.

John had introduced me to two of his best friends, Mark and Rick, and their wives, Donna and Saundra. I became instant friends with both of their wives.

Donna was a successful realtor, and Saundra was a registered nurse. We had a lot in common as all three of us had Caribbean upbringings.

I had called up Donna and Saundra a few days before and asked them to join me for a day of shopping therapy. We planned to meet at Brixton Market and have lunch afterward to celebrate my birthday. They were overly excited about celebrating it with me.

I told John about my plans and asked him if he had any plans for my birthday.

"I'll plan something and get back to you," he said, but he never did. I hated that sometimes he did not give me a direct answer. But I was certainly not going to make a big deal about it because that was John's way of communicating at times. I knew he would get back to me when I least expected it.

It was Saturday, the day of my birthday. I was late getting out of bed. Let us just say I had a late night. John was taking care of this love nest of mine.

I hit the shower and quickly got dressed. I was wearing my favorite blue jeans with a white cashmere sweater and my 4-inch leather boots. I could not wait to meet up with Donna and Saundra to go shopping.

I kissed John goodbye and grabbed my handbag from the closet, making my way to my car, hoping to beat the midday traffic.

When I arrived at the shopping center, both ladies were already there waiting for me.

"Sorry ladies, John kept me up late last night," I joked, and they laughed in response.

"I can see the glow in your face," Donna commented.

"And the pep in your step," Saundra chimed in. As usual, they had plenty to say.

We went to some of our favorite shoe stores and were soon laden with bags from our purchases.

"It's time for lunch; my stomach is grumbling," Donna said, and Saundra and I agreed that we were both starving after spending all that time shopping.

Saundra suggested that we have Jamaican food, and I happily agreed. We walked into a colorfully decorated Caribbean restaurant, which immediately reminded me of home. We chose a nice-sized booth, ordering our food as soon as we sat down. Saundra suggested that each of us order a different dish from the menu and share it among us.

"That is a clever idea," I said. We ordered curried goat, jerk chicken, oxtail, and rice with peas. For a beverage, I opted for an ice-cold Red Stripe beer, and my friends each chose a glass of red wine.

We laughed and chatted as we waited for our meals to arrive when Saundra's cell phone started ringing. As she spoke to the person on the line, a big smile grew on her face.

Donna and I were curious about the phone call, so we tackled her, trying to find out who was calling.

"That was my husband," she said. "He's joining us for lunch, which is unexpected."

We continued our girl talk as we waited patiently for our lunch, which took longer than we expected.

CHAPTER 5

After waiting for more than forty-five minutes, the server finally came over to our table with our food on a rolling cart. There was a lot more food on the cart than we had ordered. I did not say anything until she proceeded to place everything on the table.

"Excuse me, I said. We didn't order these extra dishes."

"I know," she said, smiling,

"So why are you placing them here?" I asked.

"A gentleman called on the phone and enquired if there were three lovely ladies here with lots of bags, having lunch in our establishment. He was able to describe what one of you were wearing, and I was able to confirm with him that you were here, and he ordered additional food for you ladies."

We looked at each other and assumed it was Saundra's husband Rick because he would be joining us soon.

We were about ready to dive into our meals when someone said, "Not so fast, wait for us."

We looked around, and there was John, Mark, and Rick walking towards us, with big smiles on their faces. I smiled. I was not expecting John to come here at all; it was undoubtedly surprising.

They joined us at the table, and we started passing the dishes around. The food was delicious; we ate our meal until we were filled. Then we lingered at the table, chatting, and joking with each other. The men, as usual, mouthed each other. It felt good to celebrate my birthday with all my best friends and my husband.

Clink! Clink!

John tapped on his wine glass. He had a big smile on his face. All of us turned our attention towards him, puzzled about what he was up to.

"I just want to say happy birthday to my beautiful lady, Desaray. I am glad that my friends are here to help me celebrate such a special occasion. So, without further ado, let us sing 'Happy Birthday to my lovely wife."

I saw the confused looks on my friends' faces, but no one said anything. I blushed because I was not expecting John to announce that we were married.

After they finished singing, John stood up again. "I have something special that I want to say to my wife."

John knelt by the booth, holding my hand in his. He took a small box from his jeans pocket, and I covered my mouth to stifle my excitement.

John slowly peeled away the gift wrap and opened the tiny box which held the most beautiful one-carat diamond ring. I let out an ecstatic scream, unable to withhold my excitement.

"Desaray, will you accept this ring from me to you?" I knew it would sound like a strange proposal to my friends, but John and I would explain later.

"Yes!" I squealed, embracing him close to my body. "Yes, baby, I will accept," I said, giving him a juicy kiss.

Donna, Mark, Rick, and Saundra got up from the table and hugged us both.

"We are so happy for both of you," Donna said.

"Yes, we are," the rest of them chimed in.

"But why didn't you ask for her hand in marriage?" Saundra asked.

John said, "I need to explain our little secret to all of you. Desaray and I have been married for over two years now. We got married at the registry so that Desaray could stay in the country legally. At that time, I promised Desaray that I would give her a formal proposal when the time was right. I figured the best time to do it was on her birthday. I knew she would be surprised because she wasn't expecting it," John explained.

"Oh, that's so sweet," Donna said.

"I am looking forward to having a nice wedding too," I hinted. I was hoping that John heard me loud and clear. I did not want to wait another two years to have that intimate wedding he promised me.

"There is something else I need to say to Desaray," John spoke out.

I looked at him, wondering if there was another surprise up his sleeve.

He handed me an envelope and asked me to open it and read it aloud. I was hesitant, but I did as he asked, "Desaray Lawrence, you have been enrolled in our autumn semester class starting on September 5th, 2004, at Sassoon Academy for hairdressing."

I covered my mouth, unable to speak. I looked at John, and he smiled as I hugged him. "Thank you, baby, for doing this for me! I am so grateful."

"Can you please explain what is happening?" Donna said.

"John enrolled me at Sassoon Academy to take courses in hairdressing!" I said excitedly. "We spoke about this a while ago and I thought he had forgotten!"

"That is nice of you, John," Saundra said, and the rest of the party agreed.

John amazed me more.

CHAPTER 6

I had never felt so happy in all my life. This was made possible by John. I was doing well at the academy and was looking forward to completing my studies and starting work.

The time went by so quickly, and soon eighteen months had passed, and I was ready to start working on my own. I completed my NVQ Level 3 in Hairdressing at Sassoon Academy. I was enormously proud of myself for all the commitment and dedication I had put into the courses.

I wanted to celebrate my accomplishment with my friends, so I asked them to meet John and me at Chishuru Restaurant for a celebratory dinner. We laughed and chatted throughout dinner, enjoying our time together.

Donna, who was sitting across from me, congratulated me again. She then asked me if I was going to work for myself or collaborate with an employer.

"I plan to rent my chair. Girl, I am so excited to start my new journey! And can you believe I even started looking at salons already and found a nice spot close to Brixton Market?"

"Really?" Saundra said.

"Guess who is going to be my first client?" I laughed.

"Who!?" Donna started giggling.

"You and Saundra, of course!" I laughed.

"You mean we are your guinea pigs," Saundra said jokingly.

"Get out of here," I said, as the three of us started laughing at our jokes.

The West African restaurant certainly lived up to its reputation; our meals were excellent.

It started raining as soon as we left the restaurant. It was pouring and chilly as John pulled into the garage, and he closed the door quickly to keep the cold out. I turned on the light as we entered our home, and John immediately turned on the electric fireplace to warm the house up. I changed into my silk nightgown after I freshened up, and I joined John by the fireplace.

John pulled me in his embrace, kissing me softly. "Honey, you have come a long way, and I am so proud of you," he said.

"Thanks, baby," I answered.

"Let me show you how proud I am," John said, and pulled me onto his lap, kissing me deeply.

My body immediately reacted to his kisses and tender touches. "Somebody is ready for some action," I whispered.

"Yes, honey, I want to give you some of this good stuff," John responded with a deep groan.

He got up from the sofa and led me closer to the fireplace, and we laid on our blankets on the carpet. He pulled me close; our warm bodies pressed up against each other. We kissed passionately, enjoying the sparks that lit up or burning bodies, awaking our desires.

My body reacted to John's every manipulation. I was ready to release it all, every emotion, every hurt, every pain that had kept me silent for years. I had never known love like this existed. But for sure, this man took away all my fears and kissed my pains away.

I screamed at the top of my lungs, shocking him in the process, but this was my release. I could finally let go, free from the darkness that had been keeping me a prisoner in my own body.

I got up early the next morning and made John's breakfast. I wanted an early start at the beauty salon. I put all my accessories into my pull-on bag and headed out. I parked my car in the first available parking space and walked towards the salon.

The gentleman that owned the salon was just opening the door. We had not met in person before.

"Good morning," I said in a chirpy voice. "I'm Desaray."

"Nice to meet you. I'm Murray," he said, shaking my hand.

He showed me around the lovely salon again, he had made some changes to the interior, and it looked so much better than the last time I was here. He showed me my station. It was very elegant. He had certainly made a lot of changes to the salon, and I loved it. I placed all my hair products and equipment on my station. I was excited to start my day.

Saundra was my first client, and I hoped this would eliminate some of my fears because she was my friend.

At exactly 10:00 a.m., Saundra came through the door and sat in my chair. "Are you ready to perform miracles on my hair?" she laughed.

"What are you getting done today?" I asked her, sounding all professional.

"Girl, I need a perm and a rinse, and don't go all bougie on me," she said with a laugh.

I also laughed, knowing Saundra was just being silly.

"Please make sure you do a decent job," she warned jokingly.

"Wait until I am finished, then you'll be able to give me your opinion, "I said.

My skills and training had paid off. When I turned Saundra's chair around for her to see my handy work, she was blown away. I must admit, I was proud of myself.

"Girl, you did an excellent job with my hair and the color; it's the bomb!" she said excitedly.

"Did I pass the test?" I enquired with a wide smile.

"You certainly did, and I am not saying that because you are my friend."

"Please refer your friends," I said to her.

"I certainly will," she answered.

For the rest of the day, I was kept busy with walk-in customers. I saw the potential for me to make money at this location and was even more driven to achieve my goals.

As I was about to leave at the end of the day, Murray popped up again and asked if I had had a good day.

I told him I did. "So, I'll be seeing you tomorrow?" he asked.

"Yes, I'll be back; your salon is a precise fit for me," I said, smiling at him.

After having such a busy day at work, I was exhausted. As soon as I got home, I flopped down at the dining room table.

"Baby, I'm home," I called out to John.

"How was your day?"

"Tiring, but everything went well," I responded.

"I made dinner for us, so relax, and I will serve you, honey," John said.

"Okay, I am *starving*," I said with a laugh.

I enjoyed the tasty meal John had prepared for dinner. He was such a good, and I loved him so much.

"Would you like a foot rub after your shower?" he offered.

"Honey, which would be perfect. I could do with one." I kissed him tenderly on the lips.

After my shower, John rubbed and massaged my feet. The foot rub was so relaxing I fell asleep on the sofa. I woke up later in the night with a blanket thrown over me.

CHAPTER 7

Business at the salon was going well. I rented two more chairs as my clientele grew bigger. I also presented some ideas to Murray on how we could increase sales, and he liked all my ideas.

Murray asked me to sit with him one evening after work and asked me to give him more details on my ideas. I told him that we could incorporate services such as eyebrow waxing, eyelash extensions, and makeovers, and he could also hire a manicurist.

He loved my ideas and offered me a business partnership. He explained the terms of our partnership. We would share the profits from the new services that we would be incorporating.

I told Murray that I would love to be his business partner if our prior arrangements were still in place. That is, I would still be an independent contractor. I would continue renting my chairs, and my customer will remain as mine and not part of this partnership. He agreed to our arrangement, and that was how we became business partners.

I loved being my boss; it gave me so much independence. I was earning my own money and was able to contribute towards our bills at home. This was a milestone for me.

During the winter months, I realized that the salon was slow. I implemented at-home services, and my customers loved the convenience. This service paid me significantly more, and with this added income, I was able to work fewer hours during the winter season.

I was saving most of my money from the salon in my business account and was amazed at how quickly my savings had grown. I looked at the bank statement several times, amazed that I had saved so much in a brief period. With all this money in my bank account, my mind wandered back to my homeland, Jamaica. John and I had been discussing building our dream home back on the island for a while, but John still had some reservations. I hope to change his mind if I can show him that I am to contribute to building our house in Jamaica. I had more than enough money saved to put with him to buy our plot and start building.

I had to paint a picture for John, and I was good at doing so. As we sat at the table after dinner chit-chatting. I approached the subject again, asking John to let me explain my thought process.

"John, I had always wanted to have a house but never had one. My dream is for us to have a house that overlooks the ocean, our piece of paradise. During the winter, it can be our getaway. Whenever we do decide to move to Jamaica, we will have a home there waiting for us." I also explained to John that I had saved up enough money to help with the purchase, trying my best to put his mind at ease.

John finally relented, and we planned our trip to Jamaica.

Our trip to Jamaica was supposed to be all about business, but I could not be on the island and not have some fun. I let out the deep breath that I had been holding when the aircraft touched the ground, and calmness filled up my entire body. All my anxiety was gone.

My mother did not know I was coming to Jamaica. I knew she was going to be surprised to see us and excited to meet John in person for the first time.

I never realized how much I missed Jamaica until we started driving through the streets. "I am so excited!" I said, turning to my husband.

"I can tell you are, honey," he said.

"Baby, I missed the blaring reggae music, the smell of jerk chicken roasting in the jerk pans along the roadside. The vendors in the market selling their produce. And what I missed most was the wide variety of fruits that are grown here. I missed the sweet, juicy apples, mangoes, oranges, pineapples, sugar canes, and my favorite fruit, sweetsop. I loved driving in the countryside smelling the fragrance of the flowers and plants that grow by the wayside," I reminisce.

I was home, and I wanted John to have a better experience than the one he had when he previously first visited the Island. I planned to show him our beautiful island with its white sandy beaches. Expose him to our culture and for us to just bask in the sun as we lay on the beach, listening to the waves as they come ashore. And most of all, just enjoy these moments together, forgetting all other worries.

John and I went straight from the airport to my mother's house. I called her on the phone and told her I was outside.

"Outside!? Desaray, stop playing games," she said.

I saw the door open slowly, and she peeked her head out. When she saw John and me, she screamed and ran into my arms, hugging me so tightly, tears streaking her face. Making me tear up too.

After she gathered herself, I introduced her to John. "John, this is my mom, Olive. And Mom, this is John."

John gave her a brief hug and said, "It is nice to finally meet you in person after speaking to you so often on the phone."

"It's my pleasure to meet you too, John."

My mother welcomed us, inside the house and John, and I spent two amazing days with my mother. We ate, laughed, and talked for hours.

John and my mother got along very well, and my mother was overly impressed with John. It was sad when we had to say our goodbyes. Our stay was short, but we had a wonderful time being there with her.

We then headed to the Wyndham all-inclusive hotel to spend the next three days before heading back to England.

We decided to use the following day to enjoy ourselves, swimming in the ocean and walking along the white sandy beach. We sipped on cocktails, soaking up the sun while lying in the lounge chairs along its shores.

"This is so beautiful, Desaray. I am in love with the island," John said.

"How about me?" I jokingly asked.

"Honey, you are first, the island is second," he said smiling.

The next morning, we got up early and toured the island. We found a nice plot of land overlooking the ocean.

"This is perfect," I said to John excitedly. I immediately fell in love with the location.

We took the information from the listing and went to the Coldwell Banker office located in Montego Bay. We were able to speak to one of the sales agents about our interest in buying the plot after negotiating on an agreeable price. We soon signed all the necessary paperwork and closed the deal.

We hired a contractor recommended by the agent. John gave the contractor the design he had in mind for our home and a deposit for him to start building. We agreed that John and I would make payments as he completed various stages of the construction.

CHAPTER 8

We got back to England and life was back to normal. Our heads were no longer back on the island. Our minds were now in working mode.

However, I soon learned the meaning of the phrase "It's easier said than done."

As soon as we got back to England, we started having issues with the contractor. He wanted more materials and more money, even though most of the work had not been done according to the terms of the contract.

We got rid of the first contractor and we had to get rid of the second one also after experiencing similar issues. It was becoming frustrating, and John's patience was growing thin.

We were now on our third contractor, and I took more frequent visits to Jamaica just to be on top of things. I wanted to make sure that our hard-earned money was being used to build our dream house and not squandered by contractors for their benefits.

I was also back on the grind at work and saving most of my money so we could keep up with our added expenses. John and I were in a happy space, both emotionally and financially. I had to give God thanks for blessing us.

On my thirty-fifth birthday, I came home to see a brand-new Mercedes Benz in our driveway.

I squealed, "Oh my God, baby, this is beautiful!" I hugged and kissed John as he handed me the keys to my new car.

What more could I have asked for? John was my perfect man.

"I am going to take care of you tonight, baby," I whispered in his ear.

"I can't wait," he responded, a big smile spreading across his face.

We went out that night to dinner and dancing, and we had a wonderful time. As soon as we got back home, I headed straight for the shower. I was sweaty from all that dancing, but I wanted to show my husband how much I appreciated him. I took a nice, long shower, changed into my sexiest lingerie, and posed seductively on the bed, waiting for him to get out of the shower.

John's smile widened as he entered our bedroom. His eyes scanned my body as I lay in the bed, looking hot and sexy.

"Come over here, baby, and let me give you some sugar," I purred.

He came and sat on the edge of the bed. I got up and turned the music on, swaying my hips to Marvin Gaye's "Sexual Healing," as it played from the speakers.

John stared at me while I continued my seduction. Soon, he reached out to me and pulled me into a warm embrace and slow dance with me. I could feel his rise.

"Come and sit on it for me, honey," he whispered as he laid back on the bed, his eyes locked with mine.

I took my time easing down slowly, never breaking eye contact with him.

"Honey, I love you," he whispered.

"I love you too," I whispered back.

I gave him my all, emotions that I had never shared with anyone else because my past was too painful. I had locked most of my memories away. I was too scared to be vulnerable, but John had slowly peeled away all those layers, and now I was flying as free as a bird.

CHAPTER 9

I was at home putting away some laundry when the phone rang. It was Saundra, asking if I could spare a weekend off from work. She wanted Donna and me to join her on a girl's trip to Central London.

"That sounds exciting! Give me time to reschedule some of my appointments and I'll get back to you," I told her.

I called most of my clients and re-booked their appointments. Then I called back Saundra and told her that the last weekend was in August.

It would be a perfect time for us to take a trip. Saundra said she would relay the information to Donna.

Donna called me later that evening and suggested that we book an all-inclusive hotel for the weekend.

"That sounds good to me," I said to her.

The following weekend came around very quickly. As soon as Saundra pulled up in my driveway, she started blaring the horn.

"I'm coming," I shouted, scrambling to put on my sneakers. I kissed John goodbye. "I'll call you as soon as we arrive at the hotel," I said to him.

"Have a safe trip, honey," he said.

I placed my carry-on inside the trunk of the car and sat in the back seat. "Ladies, are we ready to have a wild weekend?" I asked.

"That's what I am talking about!" Donna said excitedly.

"I am hoping that our husbands get together and do something fun," I said.

"I think they will, based on what Rick told me," Saundra responded.

We drove to the elegant Sydney House Chelsea hotel and checked into our adjoining rooms at the front desk. The hotel was beautifully decorated. I liked everything about it, especially the fireplace.

We decided to get ready and meet in an hour for dinner at the hotel's seafood restaurant. We met up in the lobby, and I must say that all three of us were looking spectacular. We had few admirers, but we were all married women.

We placed our order for the lobster special, which came with a three-ounce lobster tail, rice, and curry sauce. Red wine was our choice of drink.

"It's so nice to get away and to have a moment for ourselves without our husbands," I said to the girls.

"I am sure our husbands are thinking the same thing," Saundra said.

"At least they can watch their games without our constant interference," Donna said. We laughed at the idea that our husbands might be celebrating without us.

The lobster dinner was enjoyable. "I am so stuffed," I complained.

"I am ready to go and dance some this food off!" Donna said. We took care of the bill and then went next door to the jazz club. The jazz club was swinging, and the DJ was playing some immensely popular disco music. We started getting our groove on. We danced and laughed until our feet were sore.

"I think we should call it a night," I said. Both ladies agreed that it was time to head back to the hotel.

"I had so much fun," Donna said, and Saundra agreed.

The next morning after breakfast, we headed to the spa to get pampered. The sauna was first on our list of things to do. The mud bath would be next, and finally, the massage parlor.

While we were enjoying the mud bath, I asked Donna if things were good with her, and Mark, and she immediately said yes. I knew she was hiding something because she was too quick with her answer; It is unlike her not to do reverse psychology on me.

"Donna, if something is going on, you can share it with us. We are all friends here." It was funny knowing that I am an open book when it comes to my business. They wanted to know everything happening in my marriage. But when it comes to their personal life, it is a secret.

After a bit of prompting, she finally opened. "Mark is having problems in the bedroom," she blurted out. "I don't know if it is the stress at work, but he has not been able to perform."

"How long has this been going on?" Saundra asked.

"Since he got a new position six months ago. He was so excited about the position, which came with a nice increase. But it also came with a lot of responsibilities and headaches. Some nights he must stay there for hours after all the workers leave, trying to reset the outdated computer system which keeps chipping out. He suggested to his boss to put in updated software because the current one was no longer managing the volume of users anymore. His boss refuses and expects him to make, *A mountain out of a stone*. Whenever he gets home, he is tired and grumpy. We get into the bed, and he cannot function," Donna explained sadly.

"Have you encouraged him to seek help?" I asked her.

"Yes, but he refuses to talk about it. I am so fed up. I am just ready to move out and live on my own."

"No! Donna, you can't do that," Saundra and I spoke at the same time.

"Donna, would you be upset if I tell John about what is going on with Mark? John might be able to talk some sense into him."

"He can try," she said, "but Mark is very stubborn, and I cannot deal with his attitude and his mood swings."

"I am sorry that this is happening," I sympathized.

I asked Saundra the same question that I had posed to Donna. Saundra was always tight-lipped when it came to her business too, but I was not going to let her off so easy. "Come on, Saundra it's your turn," I said.

"Rick wants a baby!" she suddenly said.

"That's great!" I said excitedly.

Saundra did not smile or look at me.

"What's wrong?" Donna asked. "Aren't you excited to have a baby?"

"I am not ready for a child. I want to get a better position at the hospital, and a baby is not in the picture right now for me," she said.

"Can't you do both?" I asked.

"To be honest with you both, I'm not sure I want a child."

I was shocked by Saundra's statement. But I kept my opinion to myself. "I think you should discuss it with your husband, don't keep him in the dark," Donna said.

"I agree," I said. We continued our girl talk, supporting each other. We all had skeletons in our closets.

With all the drama happening in our marriages, the massage parlor was a welcome relief to relax our aching bodies.

CHAPTER 10

After leaving the spa, we went to the swimming pool and swam for a while, totally enjoying the facilities. Donna asked me if I had set a date yet to renew my wedding vows. I told her not yet, then she quickly changed the subject before I could expand on the question.

"Ladies! I am invited to a private party in the gazebo tonight. Are you both interested in going?" Donna asked.

"Sure," I said. We may as well enjoy our time here, while we can."

"Who invited you?" Saundra asked, curious as usual.

"The front desk clerk did when I ordered room service this morning. I think all three of us should wear something white tonight," Donna suggested.

"I think that's a clever idea," I agreed.

"Is 7:00 p.m. a suitable time to meet at the tiki bar?" she asked.

"Sounds like a plan," Saundra said.

I went upstairs and took a long, relaxing bubble bath. After my bath, I dried and lotion my skin. Then I took out my white, maxi, off-the-shoulder dress, which I had purchased earlier in the week, and placed it on the bed.

I placed my silver four-inch stilettos next to the bed and went into the powder room to apply my makeup. I applied my Mac foundation on my face, finished with my compact powder, applied silver sparkle on my eyelids, and painted my lips with my bright red lipstick. I must admit, my face looked flawless after I had finished applying all the makeup.

I slipped into my dress, which looked very elegant, and put on my stilettos, then adorned my neck with a silver choker. I sprayed my Hermes perfume on my skin then headed out the door with my clutch purse tucked under my arm.

I came out of the elevator and strutted across the pool area to the tiki bar, where Donna and Saundra were already waiting. I threw air kisses to both and took the available seat next to Saundra.

"You look beautiful," Saundra said to me.

"And you're glowing," Donna added.

"Thanks! Both of you look stunning also," I complimented them.

Donna pointed to the gazebo with its white, carwash-style curtains fluttering in the wind. "The party is going to be inside there," she said.

The gazebo looked amazing with its dazzling array of string lights wrapped delicately in white lace and attached to two tall pillars. It was a total transformation from how it looked earlier in the day.

We sat at the bar for about half an hour, sipping our margaritas and enjoying the cool night air. "Ladies, the party is about to start. Let us go inside," Donna said.

"What's the hurry?" I asked her.

"You know Donna, always trying to get the best table," Saundra explained.

The host greeted us as we entered the gazebo and escorted us to one of the plush white sofas decorated with blue and gold pillows. A bucket holding ice and champagne sat on a coffee table next to us. There were about eight other sofas scattered throughout the gazebo, all with the same accouterments.

"This is elegant," I whispered to my friends.

"It is," Saundra said. "It's a beautiful setting."

The DJ started playing an array of popular R&B music, setting the mood. "Come on, girls, let's go on the dance floor and bust a move," Donna said.

We went on the dance floor and started getting down, laughing, and enjoying the moment. Suddenly, someone tapped me on my ass.

"I swear! Who—" I was ready to give this person a piece of my mind, but then I turned around, and the rest of my words trailed off? "John! What are you doing here?"

"Did I surprise you, honey?" He smiled at me.

I noticed that Donna and Saundra were laughing at me. "Did you guys know that John was going to be here?" I asked.

They nodded in acknowledgment. "Mark and Rick are here also," Donna said.

"What! Where are they?" They both looked in the direction of the bar. "What's going on, girls? Why am I the only one in the dark?" I started laughing. "Is there something I need to know?"

John held my hands in his. "Honey, I have something special planned for us tonight."

John led me over to the DJ's booth and borrowed the microphone. "Desaray," he said my name in a sultry voice. "I came here tonight for us to renew our vows. I promised that I would give you your intimate wedding, and I am ready to make it happen. So, without further delay, let us do it. The clergyman is already here waiting to officiate our ceremony."

My legs were shaking; I was so nervous! I tried my best to slow my breathing down as my heart continued racing.

"Are you ok, honey? Do I need to hold on to you?" John said, chuckling at me.

"I'm ok," I whispered.

The clergyman stepped forward, followed by Donna, Mark, Rick, and Saundra, who gathered around me. My hands were shaking, and tears were filling my eyes.

The clergyman took the microphone from John and spoke into it. "People, we are gathered here to witness the renewal of vows between John and Desaray Lawrence. John, please take Desaray's hand in yours and repeat after me: Desaray, I will always cherish and love you for the rest of my life, in sickness and in health."

John held my hand in his and repeated his vows, confirming his love for me.

"Desaray, please repeat after me," the clergyman said. "John, I will always cherish and love you for the rest of my life, in sickness and in health."

The tears kept coming as I repeated my vows to John. No words can express the joy that this man had given me. This was the happiest day of my life. My husband had gone beyond to surprise me. And if that was not enough, John placed on my finger a diamond-encrusted wedding band that perfectly matched my engagement ring.

"Can we ask the bride and groom to open the dance floor?" the DJ announced. He selected one of my favorite R&B songs by Luther Vandross, "A House is Not a Home."

I could not stop crying; this night was simply perfect. John and I kissed eagerly, both of us expressing our love to each other as we danced the night away.

I had one of the most amazing weekends with my husband and friends at the Sydney House Hotel.

I was still on cloud nine when I got back home. I could not stop looking at the beautiful wedding rings on my finger. "Mrs. Desaray Lawrence," I said quietly, loving the sound of it. It just felt more official this time around.

CHAPTER 11

Murray called me while I was at home doing some chores. He was excited to know about my getaway. I explained to him that John and I had renewed our wedding vows. He congratulated me and asked if I would be at the shop on Monday. I told him I would be.

I noticed that Murray was calling me a little more often, but I did mind it. I was glad that he and I had a good business relationship and that he kept me informed about the salon whenever I was not there.

It was Friday, one of my busiest days at the salon. I had forgotten to call John on his lunch break. I was finishing my client's hair when my cell phone started ringing, but the phone cut off before I was able to answer it. I took the towel from around my customer's shoulders and told her to pay the receptionist.

Suddenly my phone started ringing again. This time I answered before it went to my voicemail.

"Hello. Is this Mrs. Desaray Lawrence?"

"Yes," I answered, "this is her."

"Are you able to come to Brixton Hospital? Your husband was just admitted here," the woman on the other line said.

"What happened?" I asked.

"He passed out at work," she said. "He was taken by ambulance to our hospital. We will give you more details when you get here," she explained.

"Oh my God, I am on my way!" I put the phone down. "I have to go," I said, asking my assistant to take care of the rest of my clients. I ran to my car, sped out of the parking lot, and headed to the hospital.

I prayed that John was all right and hoping that the police would not pull me over for speeding. When I got to the hospital, I was a nervous wreck.

"My husband, Mr. John Lawrence, was just admitted here. Can you direct me to his room, please?" I asked the nurse sitting at the desk.

"He is in room one hundred and two, down the hall, third door on your left," she directed me.

I walked into the room and rushed over and hugged John, who looked so weak, lying in the bed. Tears welled up in my eyes. "Baby, how are you feeling?" I asked.

"I'm doing well," he said, and I looked at him skeptically. "I'm still talking, aren't I?" he smiled, making light of the situation. "I had a slight stroke; it has affected my left side. I will be here for a while, Desaray," he said, wiping away a tear that trickled down his cheek.

I had never seen my husband so vulnerable. He was always such a strong person, my rock, whenever I was down. It had been only a week since we renewed our vows.

"Why, God?" I asked as tears streamed down my face.

John was sent to rehab after leaving the hospital. He was there for a couple of weeks going through therapy.

It was a very tough time for me, trying to balance taking care of John and working at the salon. Luckily, our friends Donna, Saundra,

Mark, and Rick were there for both of us. The guys visited John at the rehab facility frequently, and the ladies took me out sometimes after work. With their help and support, I was able to keep the shop running and take care of John without falling apart.

CHAPTER 12

John was released from rehab after about eight weeks. He had gone through intensive rehabilitation and his health had improved, even though he was now confined to a wheelchair, unable to walk on his own without help.

I was sad that our lives may never be the same again, but I prayed that with time he would get better. I showered John with lots of love and affection, promising him I would always be there for him.

I did my best to keep John motivated especially whenever he seemed depressed, hoping that I could lift his spirits, but John was still hard on himself. "Desaray, I am not the same man you married" was his new phrase."

It stressed me out to hear it because I was still struggling to figure out our new normal. "Baby, you are still my husband; I love you. We'll get through this," I continued to assure him.

At times I worried about our lives moving forward, but I still held on to my faith that with time John would get better.

Murray became my sounding board during this time. He would listen to all my complaints, assuring me that with time John's health would improve if he continued with therapy. I was drained, mentally and physically. I prayed that God would just give me back my vibrant and loving husband.

John and I began arguing a lot. I was fighting my own battle internally, trying to deal with our situation. John's health had taken a toll on me emotionally, and I was tired, stressed out, and not sure how to deal with our issues. I tried to be optimistic and not focus so much on John's disability, but at times it was extremely hard.

Today had been a long day at work for me, and I was ready to go home. I locked the shop door and headed to my car. The sound of a car horn alerted me. And then I heard someone calling my name.

"Desaray!" the person called my name again. I looked around and saw that it was Murray.

"Desaray I am going to get something to eat, do you want to join me?"

"Sorry, I can't. I need to get home to John," I said, politely rejecting his offer.

Murray was persistent. "Come on," he said. "I know you must be starving; let me treat you to dinner. If it will make you feel better, call John and let him know you are having dinner with me."

I called John and told him I was having dinner with Murray. I told him I would be home in another hour or two. He told me to have fun.

"Love you," I said at the end of the call.

"Me too," he responded.

Murray and I ordered the salmon dinner special at Zito's, an Italian restaurant. We hung around for a while and had a couple of drinks. I felt like myself again as I listened to the jazz music blaring through the speaker. This was one of the spots where John and I spent a lot of time together. I smiled, reminiscing about the last time John and I were here; we had had a lot of fun.

I was noticeably quiet driving back with Murray to pick my car up from the salon parking lot.

"Are you ok?" Murray asked.

"Yes, I'm ok, just lost in my thoughts," I said.

Murray pulled up alongside my parked car. He came around to the passenger side of his car and held the door open for me to get out. I stumbled a little and he held on to my arm and asked if I was ok.

"Yes, I am ok," I said.

Murray pulled me in his arms and kissed me softly on the lips. I was astonished by his gesture, but my head was fuzzy, and I did not do anything to stop him. I wanted to say something but could not get my words out.

Murray kissed me again, this time more intensely. I kissed him back. I do not know if it was the alcohol, but I enjoyed his kiss a bit too much. I was caught up in the moment, and my body started to react in a way I never expected it to.

I broke away from his kiss, realizing that I must be drunk or something. Thoughts of regret immediately rushed into my head.

"I had a wonderful time hanging out with you, Desaray," he said.

"I am sorry, I need to go. I don't know what got into me," I said nervously. "Good night."

I drove away, leaving Murray standing in the parking lot. My mind was still on the kiss Murray and I had shared and how good it felt. Part of me longed to feel those feelings again.

"What the hell were you thinking, Desaray?" I kept asking myself as I drove home. "You need to get it together."

I sat outside in my car for a while before entering my house, trying to clear my head. When I walked in, John was waiting up for me.

"Honey, did you have a fun time?" John asked.

"Yes, I did, baby, thanks for waiting up." I was unable to look my husband directly in his eyes.

CHAPTER 13

A month later, I told John that Murray and I had kissed.

"What did you say, Desaray?" John shouted at me.

I repeated myself. "But, honey, I can explain. That kiss meant nothing."

"Nothing, Desaray? You kissed your damn business partner and said it was nothing!?"

"I am sorry, baby; it was a lapse in judgment. It will never happen again," I plead my case.

"Desaray, tell me the truth. Why did you do it? So, I can understand what is going on in your head."

"Baby, you and I are so distanced from each other! You are not loving and sweet anymore. You sit around here complaining about what you are not instead of trying to be who you were. And that is being my damn husband!" I screamed. This was the first time I had to use a curse word at my husband, and I felt bad.

My outburst must have affected John considerably because he started sobbing. I walked over, sat in John's lap, and hugged him tightly, telling him how sorry I was about what had happened with Murray.

I held him until he cried out all his pent-up frustrations. I knew it was hard for John to accept the fact that he was now committed to a wheelchair and that I had allowed another man to violate me.

After John got himself together, we talked civilly about what happened between Murray and me. John said he did not feel comfortable with Murray and me being business partners, but I assured him that it would never happen again.

John said he would forgive this time because he felt that he had pushed me into another man's arms. He reiterated that kissing Murray should never happen again, and I agreed. "It won't," I guaranteed him.

What happened between me and Murray almost jeopardized our business relationship, and I could not let a situation like this risk everything I had worked.

The next day John called the shop and threatened Murray, warning him to keep his hands and mouth off his wife. If not, he would personally come to the shop and kick his ass. I knew my actions hurt John, and I knew I would never cross that line again.

I was getting ready to head home after a less than exciting day at work. The weather did not help because it rained most of the day. I went by Murray's office to tell him I was about to leave when he asked me to have a seat. I sat in the chair facing him and he opened a bottle of champagne and poured me a glass.

"Are we celebrating something special?" I asked him.

"I would say so," he responded. "The salon has made a nice profit this quarter."

"Really?" I exclaimed with excitement in my voice.

"There is a check-in this envelope, and it's yours," he said, handing it to me.

Inside the envelope was a check written out for three thousand pounds. I could not have been more pleased.

"Thank you," I said. The check was right on time because I had to send money to the builder and my mother in Jamaica. I dreaded taking money out of our savings account unless it was necessary.

CHAPTER 14

I had to run down to Jamaica to take care of some pending issues regarding my house. I intended to fire the builder if he was still dragging his feet. I was tired of the bullshit, dealing with all those unreliable contractors. I was worn out, and I figured a break from John would help, and hoping this trip would help me refocus.

After arriving in Jamaica, I took a taxi from the airport to my mom's house. I had not seen her in a while. I knew she would be surprised because I did not tell her I was coming to Jamaica. I just needed to hug mom and spend time with her. I do not know if it was the stress of dealing with the house and John's health issues, but I was very depressed.

The taxi driver drove right into my mother's yard. He unloaded my bags, collected his fare, and drove away.

I banged on the front door of my mom's house, and I could hear her asking, "Who is it?" She sounded annoyed. "Who the hell—" she yanked the door open.

"Mom!" I rushed into her arms.

My mom was speechless. She had this astonished look on her face, and her eyes were misty as she held me tightly. "I am so glad to see you, my daughter."

We embraced each other for quite a while, and both of us started to tear up.

"Desaray, are you trying to kill me? My heart is not strong enough to deal with you showing up like this," she said in her native language, a smile spreading across her face.

"No, Mom! I just wanted to surprise you," I said. My heart was filled; it felt like all the stress I had been carrying suddenly lifted off me. I missed the close-knit bond she and I shared when I was living here in Jamaica.

"Are you hungry?" she asked.

"Mom, I am starving."

We went inside, and she shared two plates of curried goat with white rice and placed it on the table.

"I have lemonade, your favorite drink." She chuckled. "It's just the way you remember it, made with lime and brown sugar," she said.

We sat at the kitchen table like old times, chatting and laughing while enjoying our mouthwatering meals.

"This feels like old times," I said to her, a warm feeling filling me up.

My mom and I talked for hours. She wanted to know about John's progress, and I explained everything to her.

"Tell John I am praying for him, and God will work everything out," she said.

"I will tell him, Mom, and I am sure he would love to hear that you are praying for him."

She then changed the conversation and asked me about the house I was building here on the island. I told her about all the problems I was experiencing with the builders.

"Desaray, are you sure you want to come back to live in Jamaica?" she asked me.

It was a strange question, and I felt a sense of disappointment. I was not expecting this type of reaction from her. "Mom, I thought you would be happy that I am settling here. We would get to see each other every day, like it was before I emigrated," I said to her.

"Des," she said, It would be my greatest pleasure to have my only daughter staying close by. But Des, people here are not the same, it is not like when you left here and went abroad. Things have changed. Some of the people living here, they cannot be trusted!" she said, a hint of sadness in her voice.

"Mom, don't worry, everything will be ok. I just need to find another contractor to finish my house," I said.

"Ok, my daughter, I love you. Just be careful, that is all."

A chill ran through my body. I was not sure why.

I went to see my new house, curious to see the progression. It looked more beautiful than I had anticipated. Most of the bedrooms were almost completed, and it seemed like things were moving along. Based on the progress I saw, I thought that it was best to keep this new contractor.

My brother Steve had suggested that I get someone to stay on the property to prevent people from stealing and vandalizing our house. He introduced me to a man by the name of Zander. He seemed like a decent person, so I interviewed him at the house.

"Miss D, I will take very diligent care of the lawn and garden for you. You won't be disappointed with my work," he said confidently.

I gave him an advance toward his pay and hired him on the spot. I then went inside the house to speak with Collin, the contractor. I told him I was incredibly pleased with the progress he had made to the house. He explained to me that most of his challenges were finding dependable workers. I told him I understood because the house should have been built by now.

"Ms. Desaray, I think I can finish building the house before Christmas," he said.

"Ok!" I said. I was not holding my breath on that promise.

CHAPTER 15

My flight back to England took longer than usual due to delays at the airport. I was overly excited and optimistic about the progress on the house and could not wait to tell John about it and show him all the pictures I had taken. So, this delay did not dampen my spirit one bit.

John was waiting up for me when I got home. I gave him a big hug and kissed him sensuously, telling him how much I missed him.

"I missed you too, honey," he said.

After sharing the news about the house with John, I headed to the bathroom to relax in my bathtub. I eased into the foaming bubble bath and rested my head against the edge of the tub, letting the warm water soak my exhausted body. God knows I needed it after such a long day.

I must have spent about half an hour unwinding before I came out. I removed a clean towel from the closet and dried my skin. I then searched in my chest of drawers for something to wear and chose a silky Victoria's Secret nightgown. I sprayed some lavender body spray on my neck and walked back to the den to spend some quality time with John. He sat in his wheelchair by the fireplace, having his favorite drink, rum, and coke. I sat on the sofa next to his chair.

"How was your bath?" he asked.

"Baby, I feel so refreshed and relaxed. I needed that after such a stressful flight," I said.

"Honey, I am so sorry you had to spend all that time at the airport. It's never easy," he sympathized with me.

I told John everything about the house and showed him the pictures. I also told him that the contractor was having trouble finding dependable workers, but I was very hopeful that the house would be ready by December.

"On a more positive note, the house is looking beautiful, even though it is not ready," I explained. "Baby, can you imagine? We will be able to take vacations and not stay in a hotel whenever we visit Jamaica. We'll have our dream house a few steps away from the beach," I said enthusiastically.

John smiled at me. "Honey, I can hear your enthusiasm, and I am delighted that you're happy. All that money we're spending on this house, it should look like a hotel, but our private hotel," he said in a devilish tone.

I got up from the sofa and plopped myself on my husband's lap, wrapping my arms around his neck and kissing him forcefully. It had been a while since we had made love. I wanted to celebrate my excitement, and I was in the mood for some loving.

I slid my nightgown off my shoulders, giving John access to my naked skin. John teased me with his sensual soft kisses along my back. I groaned, enjoying the moment. Feeling his rise, I adjusted my position, allowing access.

I backed up and ground my hips slowly, allowing John to take control of the situation. John never missed a beat, taking me to the pinnacle, igniting that fire within me.

He reminded me of the John that I knew in the past. His prowess was unmistakable, showing me that he was still the man I married. Taking care of business whether he was standing on two feet or sitting down. It was still within him, making sure both of our needs were met. Our dry spell was now ignited.

CHAPTER 16

It was Saturday, and the salon was buzzing. I was fully booked now that I had such a big clientele. At times it was overwhelming, but I loved that Murray and I ran a successful business.

John and I were finally enjoying our arduous work. Our relationship was back on track, John was happier, and so was I. We had gone through a rough patch in our marriage, but I was thankful that we were now in a better space.

After my last customer left for the day, Murray invited me to dinner. We had not been out since the night we shared that kiss.

"Give me a moment to call and tell my husband," I said.

John was fine with me going to dinner with Murray. He said he trusted that I would not repeat what had happened before.

We were in a good place. I would never allow myself to make that mistake again. I loved John and knew that I would never hurt him in that way ever again.

After we got to Billy's Pub, Murray ordered hamburgers and home fries for both of us. He also ordered a pitcher of beer for us to share.

"Did they ever finish building your house in Jamaica?" he asked, starting the conversation.

"It's not quite ready. I'm estimating it's going to be a couple more months before it will be move-in ready," I explained.

"I am proud of you," he said. I know it must have been exceedingly difficult for you to balance all these projects and take care of John at the same time," he said.

"It was! But in the end, it will be worth it," I replied.

"Is it worth it?" he asked, his voice serious.

"Yes, it is worth all the headaches and stress because, at the end of the day, it's our dream home." I was wondering where his questioning was coming from.

"If you ever need me to help you financially, just say it," he said matter-of-factly.

"John and I are good," I said. I knew Murray would help me in a heartbeat, but John would never agree with me taking Murray's money to invest in our house. *No way, Jose.* It was not going to happen. "This hamburger and fries are good," I said, steering Murray away from that conversation.

"Yes, they are," he said nonchalantly.

I realized his mood had changed, so I was ready to call it a night

CHAPTER 17

I took my pocketbook and my keys from the drawer and walked over to Murray's office. I knocked on the door to let him know I was leaving. Murray was busy tabulating the receipts for the day.

"I'll see you on Wednesday," I said. He lifted his brow with a funny frown on his face. "I have already canceled all my bookings for Tuesday," I said, ignoring his scowl.

"Is everything ok, Desaray?" he asked.

"Yes, everything is good. I just want to spend some time with my husband," I said with some attitude.

"Desaray, I love you," he said.

I was surprised. I knew he was attracted to me, but to love me was ridiculous. "No, you don't!" I said to him.

I knew Murray had feelings for meted to me, but I played ignorant to his side comments. I did not want him to get the wrong idea. Murray would try to go out with me on every occasion if I allowed him. I had seen the way he looked at me at times with such desire in his eyes.

"Can I say something, Desaray?" he asked. "I am not trying to disrespect your marriage, but if things do not work out with you and John, just know I am here waiting."

I did not respond. I was busy thinking about John. I could never walk away from John; he was my husband, and I loved him. I had accepted our fate and despite John's disability, I would never leave him for anyone and that included Murray.

"That's a very nice suggestion, Murray, but I love my husband, and I would never leave him," I said.

I could see the disappointment on Murray's face, but there was nothing I could do or say to make him feel better.

"OK, I'll see you on Wednesday, bright and early?" Murray said, ending our conversation.

On Sunday morning, John and I got up early and attended the 10:30 a.m. service at church. It had been months since we had been to church. I knew Pastor Brown would be surprised to see us. I was happy to see how much the congregation had grown since our last visit.

All of us were looking for divine intervention in our lives and I was glad God intervened when Murray tried to court me. To be honest with me, since Murray had told me he loved me, I had been thinking about it. I did have some feelings for Murray, but not deep enough feelings to leave my husband.

Thank you, God, for blessing me with a good husband and for helping me to get rid of these feelings and thoughts., I silently spoke with God.

Pastor Brown's sermon touched me in many ways. He encouraged us to be introspective when he asked the congregation a remarkably simple question, "How many of you have given up church because you have no time? No time, not even for yourselves? We give priority to everything else, but the church is often our last resort. How many of you church members agree with what I just said?" he asked.

Some of the church members held their hands up, including me. I knew that message was meant for me. I was always busy working and running around, trying to get stuff done. On Sundays, I was too tired to get out of bed, not having the energy to make it to church.

I said a silent prayer, asking God to forgive me, and I made a promise to God that I would start serving him better.

After church, John and I drove into the parking lot of Rocky Way restaurant. Today I would be treating John to the finest meal on the restaurant's menu.

Our server escorted us to the outdoor area with an amazing view of the river. John looked so happy, and it warmed my heart to see him in this happy space.

"This is romantic," John said.

"It is," I responded. "Baby, look at the menu and see what you want to eat," I said.

I was excited to be here with John. It had been a while since we had been out to a nice restaurant. I was so busy working we hardly went out anymore.

The server came back to our table. "Can I get you guys something to drink?" he asked.

"I'd like a shot of Jack Daniels on the rocks," John said.

"I'll have a glass of your Moscato wine," I chimed in.

"Are you ready to place your orders?" the server asked.

"Yes," John responded. "I'll have the T-bone steak with a baked potato and the house salad."

"And you, madam," the server turned to me.

"I will have the grilled lobster with yellow rice, the Caesar salad, and please bring me extra butter for my lobster," I said.

The server left, and I reached across the table and took John's hand in mine, caressing it gently. "Baby, I just want to tell you how much I love and appreciate you. I know I haven't said it a lot lately, but baby, you are the best thing that has ever happened to me."

My words must have touched John in a way because his eyes watered up.

Soon the server came back placed our meals on the table. "Bon appétit," he said and walked away.

John and I held each other's hands and recited a quick prayer over our food.

John cut into his juicy T-bone steak. "This is delicious," he said, chewing on a small piece. "Would you like a taste?"

"No, baby, you know I'm a seafood girl," I laughed.

We ate until our stomachs were filled, enjoying every bit of our meals. By the time the waiter came around asking if we cared for dessert, we had to decline. We had no more room for anything else.

"Can I get the check, please," I said to the server?

"Ok, madam," he said. "I'll be right back."

"Baby, it's my treat," I said to John, who protested. "I got this," I said, smiling.

"Ok," John said, giving in. "Thanks, honey, for a wonderful evening."

"Thank you for being my date," I jokingly said.

"I love you, Desaray. You are the best wife I could have ever asked for. It has been a very rough year for both of us but, honey you never gave up on me. My health has improved; I can take small steps without the aid of a wheelchair. I am feeling a lot more confident with myself. And a lot of that is because of you always encouraging me.

"I appreciate everything that you have been doing for us. Taking care of our home, running a successful business, and on top of all that, you are busy building our home in Jamaica.

"John, I did this for us."

"I am proud of you Desaray." John said.

"Thanks for being so sweet," I said.

"I am sorry, Desaray if I am rambling. I am sorry that I am not able to do the things I am supposed to do as a man and hope that with time things will get better"

"Baby, don't say that. I love you! You are the same man I married. I do not love you less." I went over to John's side of the table and kissed him gently on the lips. "John, I will always take care of you. I will never leave you."

During this moment, I realized that you could either live your life or wallow in sorrow. I was going to live my life with my husband by my side.

CHAPTER 18

The next morning, I was in the kitchen making breakfast for John when my cell phone started ringing. I scrunched up my face when I saw that the was a call coming from Jamaica. It was my contractor.

I hope everything is ok, I thought, sighing to myself. *I cannot deal with any sad news this morning.*

"Hello," I answered the call.

"Hello, Ms. Desaray. This Collin, the contractor."

"Is everything ok?" I inquired hastily.

"Yes, Ms. Desaray, I have some good news," he said.

I was still holding my breath. "Tell me about it," I said nervously. Whenever Collin called me, it was always about some problem or another. Always unwelcome news, so I was hoping this was good news for once.

"Ms. Desaray, the house will be ready by November," he said.

"Are you sure?" I questioned him.

"You have my word, Ms. Desaray," he said.

"Really!?" I said excitedly.

"I called because I need the cabinets for the bathrooms and kitchen and all the fixtures and accessories for each room. The electrician is putting in all the electrical work now, and he needs the light fixtures also.

"Collin, I've already ordered all the cabinets and fixtures for the house. Go to Scotty's Hardware and ask for the manager, Mr. Steele. He has my order. I have also arranged for the cabinet maker to install the cabinets in the kitchen. You must make sure everything was installed properly. And please, pick up the accessories for the electrician too," I said.

"I will, Ms. Desaray," Collin said. I was ready to end the call, but he spoke again, "Ms. Desaray, I have something else I want to tell you," he said, hesitating.

"What is it?" I tried not to sound too annoyed, so I let out a deep breath.

"It's about the caretaker, Zander."

"What about him?" I tried getting him to spit out whatever he needed to say.

"The other day I was at the house working and Zander said he wanted to speak to me about your house. He was asking me when the house would be ready. I told him the house would be move-in ready by December. He seemed troubled so ask him what was wrong.

"Zander responded by asking where he was going to live after I finished building your house. He was also worried about his job. He stated he did not have another available job. I laughed, thinking he must be joking because he knew this was a short-term thing, but I realized that he was serious.

"He repeated that he did not have a place of his own. So, I pointed out that he has been living here for free for a few months and that he should be able to afford to rent somewhere. I also told him he had plenty of time to look for another job. Can you believe this man, Ms. Desaray?" Collin was talking to me in Jamaican patois.

"So, what did he say after?" I quiz Collin.

"Ms. Desaray, he did not seem too pleased with my answer. He asked me to slow the work down so that we could make some extra money."

I was fuming now. "Why would this man try to sabotage me like this?" I said to Collin.

"Ms. Desaray, he was also asking me if you were married and some other personal stuff that I don't think he should be asking."

"What!?" I said, thinking that I had misheard Collin.

"I told him that was none of my business or his. I told him I was hired to work and not to pry into your business. I was getting annoyed because this man looks like he has a loose screw."

I was furious as I listened to this bullshit, but I tried to stay calm and told Collin to continue.

"Ms. Desaray, I don't trust this man, so just be careful," he warned me.

"So, what did you say when he told you to delay the work?" I asked Collin, trying to see if he planned to go along with Zander's scheme.

"I told him that I have other jobs lined up, and the longer I stayed on this job, the more money I am losing. I also told him if he needs a job when we are finished here, I can hire him if he's interested."

"This is total disrespect," I said.

"Ms. Desaray do not let Zander know I told you anything," Collin said.

"Ok," I said. "Thanks for giving me the heads up."

I was so mad that I lost my appetite. I told John he should come to the table because breakfast was ready.

"What's wrong, Desaray? You look upset. Did that phone call upset you?" John asked.

"Don't worry yourself, John. It's about the house," I said.

"Are you sure you don't want to talk about it?" he asked, offering his support.

"Maybe later, baby," I said. I kissed John on each cheek. "Baby, I am going to get dressed. I am meeting with Donna and Saundra for lunch today."

I left John at the kitchen table and changed into blue jeans, a white cotton shirt, and a flat shoe. I pulled my hair back into a nice, long ponytail. I dabbed a bit of makeup on my face and a touch of lipstick, and then I sprayed some Jimmy Choo perfume on my neck.

I went back into the kitchen and asked John if he was finished eating.

"Yes," John said. "I put all the dirty dishes in the dishwasher and started it," he explained. I bid John goodbye and reminded him that his lunch was in the refrigerator.

CHAPTER 19

I drove into the parking lot of Tropical Centre. There were a few shoe stores in the shopping center that I liked. I was hoping to pick up a pair or two before my girls arrived.

Soon my phone started ringing. I answered on the third ring. "Hello."

"Desaray, it's Donna. Where exactly should I meet you?" she asked.

I told her to meet me inside Franky's Cape.

I saw Donna as soon as she walked into the café, confident as usual. I beckoned for her to come over and join me.

"What is up, girl? We have not seen each other in months," she said.

"I know, girl just busy working. As you know, I am building a house in Jamaica and taking care of John, so I hardly have time for even myself," I laughed.

"How is business?" I asked her.

"Business has been good. I have had a couple of closings these past two months, and let me just say, I am set. Saundra called me earlier and said she is on her way."

We continued laughing and talking as we caught up on things happening in our lives. About fifteen minutes later, Saundra showed up.

"Hello! Hello!" she said excitedly, giving both of us a big hug. "How are you all doing?"

"We are good," we answered.

Saundra took the seat next to Donna. "I am ready to place my order. I am starving. I had a busy day at the hospital and hardly got time to finish eating my breakfast," she said.

I waved the server over and asked her if they had a lunch special today.

"We have a fish and chips special that comes with a free glass of iced tea," she said.

"I will have the lunch special," I said.

"Me too," Saundra said.

"I'll take the special also," Donna said.

The server delivered our food to our table, and we dug right in, not wasting any time. We were starving.

"These fish and chips are so good," I said, putting the last piece into my mouth.

"So, how is everything going with you and John?" Saundra asked.

I told the girls that Mark and Rick came by the house to hang out with John all the time, but that I hardly ever got to see them because I was always at work.

"So, Des, how is John doing otherwise?" Donna asked with a devilish smile.

Knowing Donna, she always wanted some juicy gossip, so I was already anticipating the next question.

"We are good," I said, a smile spreading across my face.

"Do you guys still do that thing?" she asked.

I pretended not to know what she was talking about. "What thing?" I asked her.

Saundra blurted out, "Sex," cutting to the chase. "I am curious, do you guys still have sex?" Saundra continued.

I pretended like I was offended by their questions. "My husband is in a wheelchair, but he is not dead," I said.

"We didn't mean it like that," Donna said.

I started laughing.

"Come on, Desaray, enlighten us. How do manage?"

I laughed again and said, "I just back that thing up and work it."

They both laughed hysterically.

"Nothing beats a good laugh," I said. I was enjoying the moment with my two besties.

"Desaray, come on, just give us a little more detail, we promise we're not going to laugh at you," Saundra asked.

"Like really," I said, knowing that these two women always wanted me to disclose information when we were spending time together. Both loved a good laugh, especially when it came to the topic of sex. "Ok," I said. "I sit on John's lap, facing him, then I wrap my legs around his waist, and it's on. Don't come knocking if you hear the wheelchair rocking," I laughed.

Both of my friends were cracking up, and I was laughing just as hard as they were. I am sure the patrons in the restaurant were thinking that we were crazy or drunk.

"So, continue with the rest of this juicy porn," Donna said, laughing her head off.

"It's always easier for us when John is sitting down," I said. "Girl, I just back that booty up, and the ride is on! We love each other and try our best to live a normal life, despite the situation," I explained to them. "Life is for living and we are doing just that."

"That is so sweet, Desaray; You are a good woman Donna said. You are running a business and taking care of John. Girl, hats off to you."

"Desaray, I know it's a lot for you to manage, but you never gave up on John, and I admire and respect you for that," Saundra said.

"Thanks for the encouragement. I love both of you. You're like sisters to me," I said.

"Ok! Ok! Let us lighten the mood," Saundra said. "Desaray, did you finish building your house back home?" she asked.

"Girl, the contractor said in three months my house will be move-in ready. I cannot wait for it to finish! It has been so much stress dealing with all the problems that come with it," I said. "I have an idea; why don't I plan a trip to Jamaica when the house is ready? All six of us will go down together, and I'll throw a big housewarming party," I said excitedly.

"That sounds great!" they both agreed.

"I have something else to tell you, girls, and I want both of you to give me your honest opinion." I proceeded to relay the conversation I had had with Collin and all the things that Zander had said.

Saundra and Donna were shocked that the caretaker would try to sabotage the entire project just to get extra money from us.

"It is such a betrayal," Donna said.

"Desaray, I don't trust that guy," Saundra said. "I think he is up to something."

"I don't know why this guy would want to sabotage everything that I have worked for. All I want is to have a lovely home for me and my husband." I started crying. "I paid this guy more than enough money to take care of my place, and this is the thanks I get," my voice cracked.

"I think you should discuss this with John," Saundra said.

"I know, I have been thinking about it. But you know how John is. He would prefer for us to sell the house, and not deal with all this headache. I think I should sleep on it before I discuss it with John."

CHAPTER 20

T he next morning, I got out of bed and headed to the shower after a very restless night. This conniving guy Zander had me messed up. Now I needed to figure out a way to tell John.

I turned the faucet on, adjusting the water temperature before I stepped inside. I just stood under the showerhead, letting the water cascade down my body.

I kept replaying the conversation I had the day before with Collin. I did not want John to start worrying about me or the house.

I dried myself off with a fresh towel from the linen closet, then brushed my teeth, put lotion on my skin, applied body spray, and went back to the bedroom to get dressed. I chose one of my jogging suits and slipped into it.

"Good morning, baby," I said to John. He was sitting at the kitchen table drinking a cup of coffee and reading the newspaper.

"Good morning, honey," he responded, looking up from the paper.

"What would you like for breakfast?" I asked.

"Some scrambled eggs with toast, please," he responded.

I whipped up a batch of eggs, toasted a few slices of bread, and laid it out on the table. I poured two glasses of orange juice and sat down across from John.

"Baby, do you have therapy today?" I asked him.

"Yes, honey. Going there at 2:00 p.m. Rick said he'll take me."

"Sounds good," I said. "John, I need to speak to you about something."

John put the paper aside and looked at me with concern etched on his face.

I told John about Zander's plot to delay the contractor from completing the house within the timeline he had given us previously. John could not believe Zander could be so dishonest.

"There is something else I need to tell you," I continued. "Zander has been asking Collin a lot of personal questions about me."

"Why would Zander be asking personal questions about you?" he asked. He seemed concerned.

"Baby, I don't know, but I will take care of it."

"Don't tell me you can take care of it, Desaray," John said angrily. First, this man tells the contractor to rip us off by delaying the work on our house, and now he is asking a personal question about you, Desaray. You don't know what is in this man's heart and what his thought process is!"

John was visibly upset; it had triggered something within him.

"Desaray," John continued. "Why don't we go ahead and sell the house when the contractor completes it?"

I was stunned, I was not expecting John to make such a suggestion. To sell our dream home. I was shocked.

"John, don't worry about that guy. I am going to make sure I get rid of him when I go to Jamaica, to do the walkthrough. The contractor told me he would be moving on to his next project when he hands the keys over to me. At that time, I will let Zander know we no longer need his services since my mom and brother will be staying at the house. Everything will be fine," I said, trying to put John at ease.

John was still visibly upset about our discussion. "Desaray, I don't feel good about this guy," he said. "I'm worried about your safety every time you go to Jamaica."

CHAPTER 21

It was the beginning of autumn, and the colors of the trees were starting to change. "I loved this time of the year," I said to myself as I laced up my sneakers.

"I'm going for a walk in the park," I called out to John. I was now spending more quality time at home with my husband, and balancing my work schedule a lot better.

I had just completed two laps around the track when my cell phone started ringing. I sat on the bench closest to me and answered the call.

"Hello, Ms. Desaray," Collin said.

A nervous smile spread across my face. I pressed the phone closer to my ear, hoping it was good news.

"Ms. Desaray, we are finally finished," he said.

I chuckled. "You're not kidding me?" I asked.

"No, Ms. Desaray, the house is ready. You can move in whenever you like."

"That's great," I said. I could not stop smiling. I was filled with anticipation. I wanted to scream, but instead, I said, "Thank you, God."

"Ms. Desaray, are you able to come down to Jamaica to do a walk-through before I move on to my next project?" Collin asked. "Any final changes that I need to take care of, I will do before I leave," he said.

"That sounds like a clever idea," I said. Let me discuss this with my husband, and I'll get back to you." We ended our call.

I was so excited! I could not wait to give John the good news.

"John!" I called out as I walked into the house.

"I'm here in the den," he said. "Honey, did something happen while you were out? You have this big smile on your face," he said when I walked into the room.

"Baby!" I said excitedly, "Our house is finally ready for us to move in."

"Really!?" John said, smiling.

"Yes! Collin just called and told me we could pack our bags and move in. I felt like a big load had been lifted off my shoulders."

"I know, honey, this is the good news we have been waiting for," John said.

"John, I have to go to Jamaica and do a final walkthrough before the contractor leaves," I said.

"Desaray, you know how I feel about you going down there by yourself," John said.

"Baby, I will be fine," I said, trying to convince them to let me go by myself. We spoke about it for hours, but he would not give in.

Later that night, I knew I had to get John to change his mind about me going to Jamaica. I convinced John to come and lay in the bed with me.

We lay there and talked about our future and how we would split our time between Jamaica and England. It was one of those special moments for both of us. We had not spoken like this in a while. This time it felt like we were one unit again. The bond and closeness that we shared when we got married had weakened after John's sickness. It seemed like we were finally going to have some smooth sailing. Now we could relax and enjoy our life.

I kissed John deeply, our tongues intertwining together, sparks ignited the flame of passion that was dormant within us. With each tantalizing touch, my body shivered.

"I am ready," John whispered.

Our bodies became as one as we rode the waves to shore. The passion between us was undeniable; Every wall was torn down as we moved through the motions. I relaxed my mind, allowing John to take me to new heights.

A tear slipped down my cheek. I did not know why I was so emotional, but the tears kept coming, but these were tears of joy. We were at the end of the rainbow, ready to share the gold between us. To start our new chapter, a life that is well deserved. All our arduous work, all our pain, all our setbacks brought us closer. We rode out the storm, and now our journey of living our best life was finally coming to fruition.

CHAPTER 22

November came around so fast. I was on a Delta flight, sitting in row 2B, on my way to Jamaica. I was filled with excitement.

I got off at the Montego Bay airport and chartered a taxi to take me to my mom's house. As we pulled up into her driveway, the driver honked his horn.

My mom came out with a puzzled look on her face. I smiled as I exited the taxi, and my mom ran into my arms, kissing my face.

"Hello, Mom," I said as I hugged her. "I wanted to surprise you again."

"I'm so happy to see you, my daughter. You can keep the surprises coming as long as I get to see you more often," she said.

I paid the cab driver, and he left. My mom led me into the house, and we sat down at the kitchen table and started talking.

My mom stared at me with a big smile on her face. "So good to see you, Desaray," she said again. "I missed you so much." Her eyes filled with tears.

"I missed you too, Mom," I said, holding her hands in mine. "Can you believe the contractor finished building my house?"

"Thank God," she said.

"Yes, thank God," I repeated. "Mom, I am going by the house tomorrow. I need you and Steve to go with me. I have a surprise to show you."

She smiled at me and said, "I hope it's a good one."

The next morning my mother, Steve, and I pulled up to my house. I was in awe. I put my hands to my mouth as tears filled my eyes.

"Mom," I said. "My house is beautiful!"

"It certainly is, Desaray," my mom said.

"Des, I am proud of you. The house is really beautiful," my brother said, giving me a huge hug.

I looked up at my house with its big French windows. The exterior was painted in a warm peach color with white trim, and the roof had grey, sloping Spanish tiles. It looked amazing.

As soon as we entered through the gate, Zander approached us. "Good morning, Ms. Desaray," he said.

"Good morning," I answered.

"Hey, Steve. And how are you doing, Miss Mama?" he said to my mom and brother.

"What's up, Zander?" my brother asked him.

I walked up the steps to the entrance of my house and knocked on the door, which was ajar. As I entered the foyer, I saw Collin in the kitchen, sweeping the floor.

"I am here!" I said excitedly.

Collin came over and gave me a big hug. "Ms. Desaray, I wasn't expecting you," he laughed.

"I know!" I responded.

"So, this is it! Ms. Desaray, your dream house is finally finished. Do you like it?"

"Oh, Collin, it's so beautiful from the outside, and I can't wait to see the rest of the inside," I said.

Collin showed us the kitchen with its beautifully designed white cabinets, black granite countertops, and stainless-steel appliances. The kitchen was so elegant.

"I am glad we used terrazzo tiles for the flooring. It matches perfectly with the cabinets," I said.

Collin led us up to the second level of the house, which had three bedrooms and three bathrooms. We stopped at the first door on the second level, which was my principal bedroom. I pushed the door open and gasped. My bedroom was the most gorgeous room in the house so far. It was an enormous room, with built-in closets, big French windows, and a huge outdoor balcony overlooking the ocean. The view was amazing.

The bathroom was my next stop, and I immediately fell in love with it. It had a jacuzzi tub and a spa-like standing shower. I had asked Collin to design the shower with wheelchair access so that John would be able to get in and out without any problem. *I know John will love this*, I said to myself.

"Everything meets my expectations. It's perfect," I said to Collin. "You did a wonderful job," I commended him.

"Thank you," he said.

"Well, I have one more surprise to show you," Collin said as he led us back downstairs.

We went through the kitchen to an outdoor patio, which led us to an adjoining walkway. And there it was, a cozy two-bedroom guest house equipped with its bathroom, living room, and kitchen. It was perfect for my mom.

I turned to my mom and said to her, "This is your little piece of paradise."

My mom looked at me, wide-eyed and with the biggest smile I had ever seen on her face.

She hugged me; her eyes all misty. "My daughter, I thank you for always thinking of me and providing for me. This is more than I could have asked for," she said.

My brother Steve hugged me too. "Sis, thank you for always looking out for Mom and me."

Collin then handed me the keys to my house and said, "Ms. Desaray, this is where we part ways. Take care of yourself and enjoy your new home."

"Thank you! You did an excellent job. I am incredibly pleased with everything," I said.

CHAPTER 23

The next morning, I got up early and made my mom some scrambled eggs and plantains for breakfast. We sat around the kitchen table laughing about the troubles I used to give her and all the lofty ideas I had in my head about moving to a foreign country.

"I see that your grandiose ideas paid off, Des, and I am so proud of all that you have accomplished." She squeezed my hand gently.

We continued reminiscing about everything, enjoying our mother/daughter moments. My mom poured us another cup of the good Blue Mountain coffee. She was still talking about how I surprised her with a new house.

"Desaray, what are your plans for the rest of the day?" she asked me.

"I am meeting the cleaner at the house at about 10:00 a.m. I will be there for about an hour," I said. "Mom, can you call for a taxi to take me to the house?"

"I have a friend who has a cab," she said. "Let me call him to get you."

An hour later, I paid the cab driver and walked up the driveway to my new house. I used my key, opened the front door, and smiled to myself. I was still in awe. I walked into the kitchen and put the cleaning supplies on the counter.

"God, I am so happy. I cannot wait for John to see our dream home," I said to myself as I looked out into the yard, admiring the landscape and pretty flower garden.

This is so amazing, I thought. My heart was filled with joy.

I heard a light knock on the door, and I turned around to see Zander coming through my door.

"Good morning, Ms. Desaray," he said.

"Good morning," I said.

He looked at me from top to bottom, a smile spreading across his face. "You look nice, Ms. Desaray," he said.

I ignored his comment.

"Ms. Desaray," he continued, "you look good in those white jeans."

I still did not respond.

"Did you hear what I just said?" he asked me.

"Thanks for the compliment," I said, giving him a fake smile.

"So, what do you think about you and me getting to know each other?" he said jokingly.

I was not amused; It just made me angry. "Listen, Zander, I am a married woman, so let's just end this conversation."

"Ok," he said, with a little attitude in his voice. "Ms. Des, do you think I can keep my job taking care of the property?" he asked me.

"Zander, I appreciate everything you have done, taking care of the property. But my mom and my brother will be staying here, and it is only fair he helps to take care of the property. Zander, you have a month to find something else. Why don't you reach out to Collin and see if he will hire you?" I told him.

"Ms. Desaray, I will take a pay cut," Zander said.

"I don't have the money to keep paying you. My brother can take care of the yard," I said curtly, unsure if he didn't understand what I was trying to say or if he was just trying to be difficult.

I started busying myself around the kitchen, hoping that the housecleaner would show up soon. I was not in the mood to keep dealing with this guy.

I wish he would just give me some space, I said to myself.

"Do you think you're better than me because you married a white man? Do you think that he is better than me?" Zander raised his voice in anger, speaking in broken English.

This guy was creeping me out. Where was all this anger coming from, and how did he know my business? I realized it must have been my brother, Steve, yapping his mouth. Didn't he know that he should not have been discussing my business?

I was getting nervous and scared, wishing that the housekeeper would just hurry up and get here. If she did not arrive soon, I decided I would leave.

Zander kept up his abuse. "Who do you think you are, rejecting me because you wed a white dude?" he continued, cursing, and insulting me and my husband.

"It doesn't matter if I am married to a Black person, white, yellow, or purple man! It is who I love. My marriage is none of your business. Who do you think you are getting into my business?" I exclaimed angrily. "I am done with this conversation. Can you please excuse me?

I have to make a phone call," I snapped, walking over to the big kitchen window overlooking the ocean.

I took the phone out of my pocket and called John.

"Hello!" John said, answering the phone on the third ring.

"Hey, baby, what's up? Are you ok?" I asked. I was happy to hear his voice.

"I am good, honey, but you sound upset," he said.

"I am upset, but not at you," I said.

"Desaray, what's wrong?" John said with concern in his voice.

"Can you believe it, John? This guy has the nerve to be questioning me about my marriage. With all I have done for him."

"Who are you talking about, Desaray?" John asked.

"Zander. Honey, why is he up in my business?"

"Desaray!" John hollered in a desperate voice. "Please listen to me; go back to your mother's house. I do not trust this guy," John said.

"But the cleaning lady—"

John cut me off. "Desaray, just go," he pleaded.

"Okay," I answered. "I love you, baby."

"I love you too, honey," John responded.

WHAP!

I was stunned. "Oh my God! John, this guy just hit me!" I cried out.

"Desaray, get the hell out of there!"

WHAP!

I stumbled against the kitchen cabinet and fell to my knees, blood spilling from my nose. I yelled out, "John! Help me! He's going to kill me!"

I started begging for my life.

"Desaray!" I could hear John yelling my name as I tried crawling toward the cell phone which had fallen out of my hand. Blood and mucus drained onto my white pants.

"Zander, please don't kill me. I am begging you," I pleaded with him.

I could still hear John screaming out my name as the phone was still on speaker. I curled up close to the refrigerator, trying to protect myself from the kicks Zander was raining down on me as my life started to fade.

"Zander, please don't kill me," I begged with every bit of strength I could muster. "I am sorry."

STOMP. STOMP.

"God, please… God, please don't let him kill me!" I cried out.

STOMP.

"Please… Zander, please, do not kill me! I am begging you."

"You are begging me now?" Zander said with a sardonic laugh. "You think you are too good for me," he said in broken English. "I took care of this property and protected it, and now you think I am not good enough to stay here? Bitch. You think because you married a white man that you are better than me?"

STOMP. STOMP. STOMP.

CHAPTER 24

JOHN

"Desaray! Desaray!" I screamed into the phone.

God, please help her, I prayed.

I was listening to my wife screaming my name, begging me to help her. This guy was killing her, and there was nothing I could do about it. She was in Jamaica, and I was here in England.

My body was numb. I was sick with nerves, unable to control the convulsions that were taking over my body. I was shaking and crying like a child. My pulse was racing, and I could not breathe.

Please, God, please do not let me have a heart attack. I could feel an anxiety attack coming on.

Breathe, John, breathe, I coaxed myself. I started breathing in and out slowly until my heart stopped racing.

"Think, John," I started talking aloud to myself. "Oh, God, help me think straight. I need to help my wife."

I unlocked my wheelchair and put it into drive. I needed to go to the den. I needed to access my computer.

I turned on the computer with shaking hands and wiped my eyes with the back of my shirt. As soon as the computer powered up, I went onto the internet and Googled "Jamaica police station," hoping they would send help to Desaray. I dialed the first number I saw on the website.

On the third ring, a lady answered. "This is Officer Kelley at the Central Police Station. How can I help you?"

"Help… help!" I screamed. "Somebody is killing my wife."

"Sir, slow down. I do not understand what you are saying. Please explain to me what your emergency is."

I started speaking more slowly. "My name is John Lawrence. I am calling from Brixton, England. My wife is in Jamaica, and I just heard someone killing her," I cried. "She was begging me to help her, but I cannot help her because I am here. Can you please send someone out to the house?" I pleaded.

"Ok, Mr. Lawrence, please give me the address where your wife is staying," the officer said.

"Oh my God, I can't remember the exact address. I know she is in Montego Bay, but I don't know where to find the address right now," I continued.

"Mr. Lawrence, I don't know where to send help for your wife without an address," she said.

"Officer, I have her brother's phone number. Please call him and see if he can give you an address."

"Did you try to call him?" she asked me.

"Yes, I have tried several times, but he is not picking up," I explained.

"I will reach out to the Montego Bay Police, and if you do find an address, call us back," the officer said.

I called Steve again, but I was still getting the same message: "All circuits are busy."

I called Desaray's mother, but the phone rang without anyone answering. I screamed into the phone, "It's urgent! Please call me back. It's John." I did not want to leave such a disturbing message on her phone because I knew it would worry her, but I was desperate.

"Lord… Lord!" I cried out. "God! Please, God, help Desaray. Please, God, save my wife!" I cried.

Where is everyone when I need help? I cursed to myself.

I continued to pray. "Lord, I don't know what I am doing. I can't go on without Desaray," I sobbed.

I was devastated. In my gut, I felt like it was too late, but I was still holding on to hope that the police would get there before she passed. She had stopped screaming after a while.

I could hear *THUD! THUD! THUD!* each time he hit her. I called her phone several times, but it went straight to voice mail.

"I need help," I screamed as I banged my fist on the table. "No, God, you can't do this to my wife. You can't do this to me!" I cried out like a mad man.

I did not know how much time had passed. When I finally got my emotions in check, I called Mark but there was no answer.

"Mark," please answer your phone. Man, I need some help. Come by the house as soon as you get this message and call me back. It's urgent."

I dialed Rick's number, the same shit.

"Where is everybody? I cannot believe this is happening," I cursed as I waited for the answering machine to pick up. "Rich, it's John," I said. "Call me. It's urgent. I need your help."

I did not have Donna's or Sandra's numbers on my phone, so there was nothing more I could do. I sighed; my body was numb, my head throbbing. I needed someone to help me.

"If Desaray were here, she would know what to do." I was talking to myself. I was losing my mind.

I went into the kitchen, and I saw a church calendar hanging on the wall. This was my final effort. I knew if I did not talk to someone soon, I was going to lose it.

I called my church to speak to Pastor Brown, and the secretary answered. "Hello, may I speak with Pastor Brown, please?" I said.

"Who's calling?" she asked.

"Tell him it's John Lawrence, and it's very urgent."

Pastor Brown came on the line. "Hello, John, what's going on? My secretary said this was an urgent call."

"Yes, pastor," I said.

"What is it, John?" he asked.

"It's Desaray… Pastor, she is dead." I burst out crying.

"John… John!" Pastor Brown called out my name. "Tell me why you are saying that. Did you hurt her?"

"No Pastor… No, she is in Jamaica," I explained. "Pastor, I need your help. I have no one to turn to."

"Listen, John. I am coming over. Please give me your address."

I gave Pastor Brown my address before hanging up the phone.

Within fifteen minutes, Pastor Brown was at my house. I opened the door and let him in.

"Are you ok, John?" he asked. "You don't look too good. Do you need me to take you to the doctor?"

"No, pastor, I just need someone to help me to figure out what I need to do."

I explained the entire ordeal to Pastor Brown, and he said he was sorry to hear the sad news. He said he was hoping that Desaray was still alive.

"John, let us pray," Pastor Brown said. "We'll pray and ask God to help Desaray in this time of need."

Both of us prayed until I felt a presence of peace and calm that filled me up.

"Do you need me to stay, or shall I get someone to come over to be with you?" Pastor Brown asked after we finished praying.

"I will be ok," I told him.

It was around 7:00 p.m. when I heard the doorbell ringing. I opened the door for Rick and Saundra and invited them in.

"What's going on, John?" they asked, both hugging me.

"It's been a devastating day for me," I said.

The doorbell rang again, and it was Donna and Mark. I invited them in, and all of us sat around in the den, and I explained the series of events, from the time Desaray got to our new house until I heard her screaming and begging for her life.

"Oh my God!" Donna cried out.

"John, I just can't believe this," Saundra said, devastated.

"Man, this is crazy," added Rick.

Mark mumbled, "This is madness."

Everyone broke down crying, and I shook my head in disbelief. All of us remained in a solemn mood but held within us the hope of getting good news.

CHAPTER 25

I t was about 6:00 a.m. when I thought I heard knocking on the front door. I sat up in the bed and listened, but I did not hear anything else.

Was I just dreaming, I said to myself? I pulled myself up on the bed rails, held on to the wheelchair, and sat in it.

I went into the bathroom, turned on the shower, and got undressed. I held onto the rails and stepped into the shower, then adjusted my shower chair and sat as the warm water soothed my body.

I started replaying yesterday's events in my head. *How could someone be so wicked? Did this guy kill my wife because he is jealous of her?*

God, I felt so useless. My wife had been screaming for me to help her, and all I could do was listen to this monster as he mocked and killed her. My tears fell again. I missed my wife so much, and I did not know if I could go on without her.

The water started to feel cold, so I lathered up my body, washed and rinsed my hair, and got out. I pulled my bath towel from the hanger and wrapped myself in it. Then, I brushed my teeth.

It was then that I realized how much Desaray did for me in the morning before she went to work. She would have all my clothes and underwear laid out on the bed for me. Now I had to do it by myself, and I just was not in the mood. I decided to put on a new pair of pajamas instead.

I had just finished drinking a cup of coffee when the phone rang.

"Hello," I answered anxiously.

"Good morning, John," Steve said. "Man, I got your message, and I went to the house and saw Zander there. I asked him about my sister, and he told me Desaray had already left and that she said she was going to visit some friends. I checked everywhere inside the house and outside. I saw no sign of her. John, it's not like Desaray to leave without telling us something," he said, his voice cracking.

"Steve, that man Zander is lying!" I screamed. "My wife called me and told me they were arguing. I told her to get out there and go back to her mother's house. She screamed out that Zander had hit her. I could hear my wife begging for her life!" My voice went up an octave, "Do you hear me? I could hear my wife screaming for me to help her, begging for her life!" I started sobbing.

"Take it easy, John. Don't run up your blood pressure," Steve said. "We are going to find her, man. John, did you say you heard my sister begging Zander for her life?" Steve asked me again.

"Yes, that's what I heard," I confirmed.

"I am going to kill that man if he touched my sister." Steve was crying as he spoke.

"Listen, Steve, do not approach him. I do not want him to know that I heard everything on the phone before being cut off. Please do me a favor and go down to the police station and ask them to start looking for my wife. Please tell them exactly what I told you. Let the police take care of this. I don't want this man disappearing," I said.

"I am going straight to the station right now," he said.

"How is your mother holding up?" I asked Steve.

"Not good, John. Since I told her about your phone call, she has been crying like she knows something bad has happened to Desaray. She is not eating or sleeping; all she does is pray. I hate to see her like this, John."

"Tell her I am sorry that I wasn't there to help Desaray," I said.

CHAPTER 26

ZANDER

Ms. Desaray came by the house, and she was looking fine. I admired her and told her she looked beautiful. I had fallen in love with her the first time her brother Steve introduced her to me. That was my secret.

I wanted to tell her about my feelings and to beg for my job. I asked her to allow me to continue taking care of the property. She told me her brother would be taking care of the yard because he would be living there with her mom.

Hearing her say this rubbed me the wrong way. She did not care that I was the one who had taken care of her property for a year.

I tried a different approach. I told her I would take a pay cut, but she still said no. I decided to push her by asking her about her marriage, and that was when she lost it.

I did not know she had that side to her, especially when I asked her if she thought her husband was better than me because he was white. She told me off, disrespecting me like I was nothing. She told me her marriage was none of my business.

Didn't she realize how much I wanted her and loved her? I was hurt. She was just using me to take care of her home, and now she wanted to get rid of me. I was boiling inside.

She turned her back on me and said, "Can you please excuse me? I have to make a phone call."

I pretended like I was leaving and waited by the door. She was speaking to her husband on speakerphone and telling him about me. He was telling her to leave and go back to her mother's house, saying that he did not trust me. I heard her telling him that she loved him, and that was when I lost it.

I walked over and slapped her in the face. She cried out, telling her husband that I had slapped her. He was screaming for her to get out of the house.

She turned around, and I punched her hard in the nose. She fell against the cabinet. She was bleeding. Her phone had fallen out of her hand, and she started screaming, begging for her husband to help her. I laughed because this man was in another country. She should have been asking me for help.

I stomped all over her body. She kept begging me not to kill her and telling me she was sorry. I was blind with fury, cursing at her. I just kept stomping on her until finally, she stopped screaming. I must have blacked out because when I looked down at her, she was not moving anymore.

She was soaked with blood.

"Shit…Shit!" I said to myself. She was dead; she had stopped breathing. I saw that there was no sign of life left in her, and I started to panic.

I saw the cell phone lying on the floor, and I picked it up. I remembered the cleaner was supposed to be coming by, so I picked up Ms. Desaray, took her out to the backyard, and laid her in the garden.

I then ran to the shed, got some clothes, and ran back to the kitchen. I started to frantically clean off the blood splatters from the cabinets and the floor with the cleaning supplies she had brought with her. Eventually, everything looked good. I felt relieved that the cleaner had not shown up yet.

I ran back outside, went to my shed, and took out my pickaxe and a shovel. I needed to get rid of her body. My nerves were unhinged.

I went back to the garden where I had laid Ms. Desaray's 'body. I dug a three-foot hole in the ground, deep enough to hold her body, and placed her in it. I took some dried leaves from the banana plants in the garden and covered her body. Then I used the shovel to fill up the grave with dirt. I smoothed the area over, and then I went back to the shed, got some cement, mixed it with some water, and poured it over the area where her body rested. Afterward, I took some more trash and laid it on top so that it looked normal.

There was no sign that anything had been disturbed. I quickly took a shower then I dumped my bloody clothing and the clothes I used to clean up the crime scene in the garbage. I poured kerosene oil on the clothing then lit it on fire. I watched as it burnt to ash.

The reality was settling in; I could not believe I had killed Ms. Desaray. My heart started pounding in my chest. It felt like it was going to jump out of my body at any minute.

I kept telling myself to calm down. Nobody knew what had happened. I started planning my escape, but I knew I had to stick around for a few more days. I did not want to bring any form of suspicion to myself. I would just act normal and if anyone came looking for Ms. Desaray, I would tell them she went to look for her friends.

The next day I continued my normal routine, trying my best not to appear nervous.

Desaray's brother Steve came by, asking me if I saw his sister. I told him she had left, saying that she was going to visit some of her friends. He asked to look around the house, and I said that was ok. I asked him if something was wrong, and he just said they were concerned because she was not picking up her phone, and it kept going to voicemail. He looked around and told me he had to go.

Remembering that I still had Ms. Desaray's cell phone, I broke it apart and threw it into the dumpster after Steve left.

On the third day after Ms. Desaray had gone missing, I was outside doing some lawn work when a police cruiser pulled up at the gate. I started to get nervous, but again I told myself to act normal.

Two male police officers exited the vehicle and came into the yard. They approached me and asked for my name, and I told them who I was.

One of the officers said, "We are here because we have had a complaint about a missing person."

"A missing person?" I repeated.

"Yes, the lady that owns this house. Her family has not seen her or heard from her since Monday. Based on the information we have received; you were the last person to see her."

"Officer, Ms. Desaray was here waiting for the cleaner. When the cleaner did not show up, Ms. Desaray left, saying she was going to visit some of her friends," I told the police officers.

They did not react in any way but said they wanted to look around and that I should wait outside. They went into the kitchen first. I hoped there was no evidence left behind. I had cleaned the kitchen thoroughly after the incident. They were inside the house for a while, then they came out and looked around in the backyard.

I guessed they did not find anything because when they left, they asked me to call them if Ms. Desaray showed up. I decided to stick around for two more days before I skipped town.

CHAPTER 27

It had been five days since Ms. Desaray went "missing." I was ready to get out of town. I packed my bag and was about to exit through the gate when a police car pulled up.

I turned around and walked back inside the house, and hid my bag under my bed. Then I went back outside to see what was up with the police coming here again. I was nervous but kept my cool as they headed in my direction.

One of the police officers asked me what my name was, and I said, "Zander." I noticed that the second officer had his hand on his gun.

The officer who asked my name said, "We need you to come down to the station with us."

"For what, officer?" I asked.

"We need to ask you some questions about the lady that owns this house."

"Officer, I already told the other set of police that came here earlier during the week what I know."

"We are taking you down to the station, so turn around and put your hands behind you," one of the police officers said.

I was about to resist when the second officer said, "Don't even try. Turn around," and pointed his gun at me.

They handcuffed me and led me to the car. The first officer who had asked for my name shoved me into the back of the police car and took me down to the station.

They took me out of the car when we arrived at the police station and put me in a private room, handcuffing my hands to the desk, and then left the room. About ten minutes later, two plainclothes officers came into the room with a folder.

"I am Detective Harvey, and this is my partner Detective Green."

I just nodded my head.

Detective Harvey said to me, "I need you to tell me what happened between you and Ms. Desaray the day she disappeared. You were the last one to see her."

"Officer, I told the police officer who came to the house that she went to visit her friends, and I haven't seen her since." My voice cracked as I spoke.

"Listen, Zander; We already know that you killed the woman. Her husband heard you killing his wife on the phone. So, what do you have to say for yourself?"

I could feel the blood draining from my head to the bottom of my feet. "I didn't do anything to her!" I denied.

The entire time, Detective Green had had a mean scowl on his face.

"Boy!" Detective Harvey shouted, "We can do this the effortless way or the hard way." He pointed his finger in my face.

"We don't want you to waste our time," Detective Green interjected. "Do you think we're playing with you? Do you think we would bring you in here without evidence?"

WHAP!

Detective Green slapped my face so hard my head spun in the opposite direction. "So, we're going to ask you again. Where is the woman's body? We need you to tell us where you put her body."

I started crying. "Officer, it was an accident," I said. Tears were now running down my face. My life was unraveling right in front of me, and I had no way out.

Detective Harvey asked me again, "Where is the body?"

"It's… it's at the house," I said.

The officers looked at each other in astonishment.

"You said her body is at the house?" Detective Harvey repeated. "Where?"

"I buried her in the backyard," I said.

Detective Green unlocked my handcuffs from the desk, yanked me up from the chair, and led me out of the room. I heard Detective Harvey telling Detective Green to request another car for backup.

Both officers led me to the police car again. Detective Green shoved me in the back seat. I hit my head on the top of the car on the way in, and my head started pounding as tears gathered in my eyes. I could feel a knot growing on my forehead.

As I sat in the back of the police car, heading to Ms. Desaray's house, I whispered to myself, "My life is over. I am going to die in prison."

I was interrupted when Detective Harvey called out my name and said, "Zander, tell me, why did you kill this woman?"

He did not wait for me to respond; He just started going off. "It's bad-minded, jealous, wicked people like you who give Jamaica a bad name. Imagine, the woman went abroad, worked hard to build her house, and a parasite like you took her life.

"It is men like you who spread hate in the community about police officers. Everybody hates the police. Yet, when they need help, the first people they run to is the police. We put our lives on the line to serve and protect, but we never get any thanks. Man, sometimes I feel like just running away from this island and going overseas because this is a thankless job," Officer Harvey said.

He continued, "We have such a beautiful island; tourists come here to experience a little bit of our paradise, and scum like you give Jamaica a bad reputation. Man, this is our paradise, and we can't even see it."

"True words," Detective Green acknowledged.

Two more police cars pulled up to the gate, and four officers walked me into the yard, holding onto my arms.

"Show us where you buried the lady's body," Detective Green said.

I led them to the back garden and stopped in front of the area where I had buried the body.

"It's here," I said.

"Where!?" they said simultaneously.

I used my feet to move away some of the trash hiding the area until the concrete slab was visible. "She is buried underneath there," I said.

"What a wicked motherfucker," one of the police officers said. I did not know his name.

"We need to secure the area," Detective Harvey demanded.

It seemed that word had gotten out that the police had me there searching for the body. A large crowd had gathered outside the gate, and they were shouting all kinds of dreadful things about me. While some were crying, others were threatening to kill me. I could hear some of them shouting at the police officers to hand me over, so they could deal with me properly.

I was more scared than ever. I was hoping the officers would not allow the community to exact vigilante justice against me. I started thinking of all the things the citizens of this community would do to me, and I shivered at the thought.

As the crowd got bigger, I became more nervous. I almost peed my pants. This was the first time I ever thought I would need help from a police officer. I hated them. But at this moment, I was glad they had me in their custody.

Detective Harvey told the backup officers to take me back to the station because he had to call forensics to come out to the scene.

I knew my life was over, and I regretted killing Ms. Desaray. I could not bear to think about what was yet to come.

"God, please forgive me," I said.

CHAPTER 28

JOHN

It was sitting in the den when I received a phone call from the Jamaican police telling me my wife was dead.

I tried talking, but my voice came out in a throaty whisper instead, and they did not hear me.

"Mr. Lawrence," the officer called out my name. "Did you hear what I just said?" she asked.

I said, "Yes, I heard you, officer. Thank you for all your help." I hung up the phone.

I put the phone back on the jack, and a gut-wrenching scream came out of my mouth. The tears ran down my cheeks. I had known in my heart that my wife was dead when I did not hear from her after I heard Zander beating her. I knew she was gone, but deep down, I was still holding on to hope.

I took a bottle of scotch from the wet bar, poured myself a stiff drink, and threw it back into my mouth, hoping it would help me numb my pain. I sat there reminiscing about Desaray and the beautiful, loving relationship we had had. I did not know what to do, so I just sat there looking out the window.

The phone rang again, and this time, it was Murray. He had been staying connected with me since he had called me two days after Desaray had disappeared. He said he was concerned about her safety, and that it was unlike her to not call and check up on the salon. He asked me if I needed his help. I told him I was good.

I did not have any bad feelings toward Murray. Desaray had asked me to let it go, and I had done.

Murray asked me if I had heard anything further on Desaray's whereabouts. I broke the news to him that they had found Desaray's body and that she was dead.

"Dead!?" Murray repeated.

"Yes," I said. "A prick killed my wife," I repeated.

Murray said he was shocked; he was not expecting this news. He asked if there was anything he could do to help.

I told him that I was good, and we ended the call. I was angry, pissed, and would kill that jerk, Zander if he were close by. I broke down and started weeping again, feeling like my world was crumbling.

Steve called me a couple of days after they found Desaray's body. He wanted to let me know they had released her body and that she was now at the funeral parlor. He asked me about funeral arrangements and if I would be coming down for the funeral.

"No. I want my last memory of my wife to be a good one. I just want to remember her beautiful face, her warm smile, and the way she kissed me before she left here. It felt so different, but a big difference if that makes sense to you, Steve. I cannot explain it, but those are the memories I want to cherish and keep with me forever. And I do not want to see what he did to her body. I can't."

I told Steve that I would wire some money to take care of all the funeral arrangements. "Please tell my wife I love her. Tell your mother hello for me. This is too painful. It's just too much for me to comprehend right now." I said goodbye to Steve and ended our call.

It was late in the afternoon when I reached out to my two best friends Mark, and Rick, and asked them to come by the house and bring their wives with them. I gave them the sad news as soon as they arrived. They were all devastated.

My next call was to Pastor Brown, asking him if he would be able to come by the house. I wanted to have a remembrance for Desaray with just our close friends.

We all sat around the big dining table in the den, talking about our fondest memories of Desaray. We laughed and we cried.

Pastor Brown said he wanted to say a few words to help us heal during this sad moment. "I know this is a very sad time for us all," he began. "Desaray is gone, and I hope she is in a better place where there is no more pain." He continued, "We all loved her, and she will remain in our memory for a long time. I will also say this to you all: make God your priority. Serve him and allow him to come into your lives. Let him lead the way and draw closer to him. Lay your burdens down and let him wash all your fears away."

Pastor Brown prayed for all of us, and we thanked him for his speech.

"I also expect to see you more often at church," he said before leaving.

CHAPTER 29

MURRAY

I called John after not hearing from Desaray for a couple of days. She normally called and asked about the shop and how I was coping, so it was strange that five days had passed, and I had not heard from her.

I was nervous as I spoke to John. I was in love with Desaray. She and I had shared a heated kiss one night after dinner. I could not stop thinking about the feelings she evoked in me. I wanted her. I wanted to make love to her and show her what I was feeling. But she had shut me down. She told me it was a mistake and that she would never leave her husband.

A month after that, while I was at work, John called and threatened me. He said that if I ever tried that stunt again with his wife, he would come over to the shop and kick my ass.

At the time, I smiled at the irony, considering John was in a wheelchair, and I did not know if that would have been possible. I did not dislike John.

He was a good man, but I wanted something that was not mine, and that was his wife, Desaray.

When John told me she was dead, it was like someone had punched me in the gut. I tried to control my emotions as best as possible while I was speaking to John. I did not want to upset him. I could not let him hear me crying over his wife.

As soon as I got off the phone, I knocked everything off my office desk. I was angry, mad, and devastated.

"If I could get my hands around that culprit's neck, I would kill him with my bare hands." I broke down. "What a loss!" I shook my head and clenched my fist tightly, trying to numb my pain.

Desaray did not even know the depth of the love I had for her, as a friend, as a business partner and if circumstances were different, I would have married her.

CHAPTER 30

JOHN

Desaray's mother called me two days after my wife was laid to rest. She said she was incredibly sad, but that she was hanging in there. She told me to stay connected and said that she would keep praying for me. I thanked her and told her I would do the same for her.

There was one more thing I needed to do to close this chapter of my life. I went into the den, sat at my computer desk, and pulled out a yellow notepad and a pen. I started to write my wife a letter.

My Dearest Desaray,

No one knows how much my heart has been broken. No one knows the emptiness that I am feeling without you here. You were my beautiful wife. I am glad you came into my life and showed me the beauty of being alive.

I never would have believed that you were going to leave this earth before me. If I had known when you left here for Jamaica that it was the last time, I would have held you in my arms and kissed your beautiful face. I would have kissed you a little longer and confessed to you, my undying love. I would have asked you not to leave me, but just stay with me a little longer. I would have pretended that I was not feeling well, so you would change your mind and stay with me.

I know you would have never left my side, especially if you knew I was sick. LOL. That is the type of wife you were, caring, kind, loving, and ambitious. No one knows what you and I have shared over the years and the love that we have had for each other. I am writing you this letter because I know how much you love reading my love letters, LOL.

Honey, you may have gone ahead of me, but I will be with you in the next life. Love you always.

Your Husband,
John Lawrence

3 MEN 1 WOMAN

All Desaray wanted was a good life and someone to love and respect her. But when love found her in a very unusual way, she took the opportunity. What was the price? And will she finally realize her dreams?

1. John- Her husband, the man she rescued and showed him kindness.

    The man who loved her and showed her what love is.

    ____

2. Murray - Her business partner and the man who would do anything for her.

    ____

3. Zander - The man with a secret obsession and a dark side.

    ____

Desaray - The woman at the center of this triangle who had three men who loves her but in their own way.

Jennifer R Scott

Three Men, One Woman

Jennifer R Scott is a single parent of two. She is from the island of Jamaica but currently resides in the USA. Jennifer loves reading and has always wanted to tell a story, using her Caribbean culture and everyday events.

She has finally decided to publish one of her novels, THREE MEN, ONE WOMAN. She has written three other books which are not yet published: DANGEROUS WAYS, MY INNOCENCE, and QUARTER TO ELEVEN.